king's vow

ELLA KADE

KING'S VOW by Ella Kade

ISBN-13: 978-1-950044-34-4 (Ebook Edition)

ISBN-13: 978-1-950044-37-5 (Paperback Edition)

Edited by: The Polished Author

Proofreading by: The Polished Author, Amira El Alam

Photographer: Xram Ragde

Cover Model: Bruno

Manufactured in the United States of America.

This is a work of fiction. Names, characters, places, and incidents either are the products of the author's imagination or are use fictitiously. Any resemblance to actual persons, living or dead, businesses, companies, events, or locales is entirely coincidental.

king's vow

We met in darkness.

Fate brought us back together and almost as quickly ripped us apart.

The world we lived in thrived on greed and deception.

Two dark souls converged and aligned in an eruption of vengeance and hatred.

Death almost ended us, and now nothing could break us. Or so we thought. What will happen when our world tries to tear us apart at every turn?

King's Vow is the intriguing first book in the Guerrera Syndicate series. If you like strong heroines, alpha males, and dark romance, then you'll love Ella Kade's mafia/drug cartel romance.

Buy King's Vow to immerse yourself in the dark world of the Guerrera's today!

arely

A GRIN TUGGED at my lips as I heard footsteps behind me. I didn't look back, but I heard plenty. Whoever was behind me thought they were light on their feet, but they were wrong. Each time I stopped at a traffic light, he slowed down and hid in the shadows where I couldn't see him unless I was trying to seek him out. No, I was going to let him think he was some 007 bullshit.

Instead of doing what most would do when they thought someone was following them, I slowed my pace. I wanted to get caught and see what would happen. Maybe, however, whoever it was wouldn't work up their nerve, and I'd make it to my destination before they got to me, or maybe just maybe, I'd have a little fun tonight.

I pulled out my phone, looking down at it, acting like I didn't know my surroundings one hundred percent perfectly. It wasn't smart for a woman to be out by herself at night in Stonewall and not have her faculties about her. It was a good thing I wasn't like most women.

The footsteps behind me quickened. It was difficult not to react as excitement built in the pit of my stomach and quickly filled my veins. I was a live wire ready to attack given the opportunity.

The footsteps came closer, and I heard the shift of fabric before I felt the slight bump. Not bad, but not good enough. I might not have noticed if he hadn't been following me for three blocks. Whoever he was, he had picked the wrong mark, and I was ready to show him how wrong he was.

In a blink of an eye, I grabbed the arm as he passed by and pulled it behind his back. He wasn't expecting my move and let out a shocked gasp before he rounded on me with his eyes wide.

I took him in. He was much taller than my five-foot-eight frame. He had to be at least six foot two or three. With his hood up, I couldn't make out much, only that he had a few days' worth of growth on his chiseled jaw and had the softest looking lips I'd ever seen on a man.

Rearing back, I pushed him in the chest with as much force as I could muster. He stumbled back a few steps and held both of his hands up in surrender.

"It's not going to be that easy," I laughed darkly as I stepped into his space. Keeping my hands on his chest, I pushed him into the alleyway in case there was anyone looking. He didn't put up a fight as I backed him up to the brick wall of one of the buildings. "Didn't your mother ever teach you not to steal from women?"

"I think she must have missed that lesson." His voice shocked me. It was deep and soothing, with a full New York accent. "Didn't your mother ever tell you to be scared of strangers in the dark?"

I yanked the hood of his sweatshirt down to get a better look at him. I wanted to see the face of the person who dared to steal from me. It caught me short at how striking he was even in the dim light. Dark, hooded eyes and dark hair cut short on the sides and lighter on the top with some curl.

I pulled out my knife and pressed the blade to his throat. He inhaled deeply but made no move to break away. Why did that turn me on? "She must have forgotten that one before she died giving birth to my brothers."

"What are you planning to do to me?" He said

barely above a whisper. With each word he spoke, his Adam's apple moved against the blade of my knife.

I tilted my head to the side. "I haven't decided yet." If he knew who I was, I was sure he wouldn't have picked me for his mark. "Why should I let you live?"

He let out a little slip of a laugh before my knife nicked his skin, and then he went still. I wasn't sure if he was even still breathing with how rigid his body went.

"You shouldn't underestimate me. I have no qualms about ending you right here, right now. You may think you can overpower me, but you can't, so don't even try. If you do, you might end up with more blood spilled."

One of his hands went for the knife. Again, thinking he was quicker than me and underestimating my speed, I dug the tip of the knife into his neck and watched as a streak of red trailed down and disappeared into his shirt.

"Fuck, lady, you're crazy."

He hadn't seen anything yet.

Leaning up, I licked the line of blood and moaned. The taste of copper and the salt of his skin had me panting. Pushing down the neckline of his shirt, I spied a small drop at his sternum and ran my tongue over the divot.

Dropping my knife, my hands went to the buckle of

his belt and quickly had his belt and his pants undone. Sinking my hand into his briefs, I gripped his cock and squeezed hard. He was so fucking hard for me. My lady boner was just as equally hard for him.

"What are you doing?" He muttered on a groan.

"Taking what I want just as you did to me." Pushing his jeans and underwear down past his ass, I squeezed once more before I let go, then I removed my panties and threw them down next to my knife. "Pick me up," I demanded.

He only hesitated for a moment before his large hands skimmed up my thighs and under my skirt. Gripping my ass, he pulled me in closer and then lifted me up. My legs instantly went around his waist, and my pussy started to grind down on his rigid length.

"Fucking hell, you're so hot and wet."

Violence turned me on. Big time. And so did he, even if he did try to steal from me.

Lining myself up, I sank down on his length, letting the feeling of being full and stretched more than I ever had before wash over me. With a dick this big, he didn't need to steal. Women would throw money at his feet to fuck him. Hell, even to his dick. For a second, I was sad I couldn't see it in the dark alleyway, and I'd never have a chance to marvel at its magnificence.

Unable to hold back any longer, I fucked him.

Taking my pleasure. My fingernails dug into his shoulders as I nipped at his jaw and along his neck. The tips of his fingers dug into the flesh of my ass, and I knew tomorrow there would be bruises. They would be the only evidence of our encounter, and soon they'd fade away.

With each rise up, I slammed down on his length, swirling my hips. I tightened my legs around him, digging the heels of my boots into his ass. I hoped I left my mark on him as well, so he'd remember me after tonight. Hell, I knew he would remember me for the rest of his days. This thief with the magical cock would never look at another mark the same way again.

He started to thrust up from under me, jerking his hips erratically. Pulling back my head, I stared down at him, tempted to bite and suck on his soft lips, but that was far too intimate. No, he would only get my pussy.

His big dark eyes looked up at me with wonder and lust while his brows pulled together.

"Stop thinking so hard. We both want this, and after tonight, we'll never see each other again."

Stilling inside of me, he closed his eyes and let out a deep groan. I could feel the pulse of his cock before he unloaded deep inside of me. If this fucker had an STD, I would hunt him down and murder him.

One hand left my ass, and with one sweep of his

thumb against my clit, I detonated. Stars filled my vision. My walls clamped down hard around his cock, never wanting the pleasure to stop. Burying my face in his neck, I bit down to stifle the scream that was building as wave after wave of ecstasy shook me to my core.

Once I came down, I sat there for a moment with my eyes closed. Damn, that was hot. Tonight would play a starring role in my future fantasies.

I tapped his bicep, and he slowly let me down until my feet were on the ground. I wanted to ask his name, but it was better off I didn't. I'd probably try to track him down if I knew.

Picking up my panties and knife, I shoved them into my purse. I wanted to relish in the feel of his cum sliding down my legs as I finished walking back to my car.

Mr. Thief, with the magnificent cock, stood there watching me. His dick was still hanging out, and even soft and in the dark, it looked spectacular.

Snapping out of his stupor, he chuckled and started to right himself. "I have to say this is a first."

"It's probably best you don't make it a habit until you learn to be quieter on your feet."

"I wasn't talking about that." He shook his head as he took me in. My breasts were still heaving. My heart galloped in my chest as I stood on the other side of the alley watching him. "That too, but I was talking about being accosted by a woman and her having her way with me."

"Well, don't worry. You'll never meet another woman like me," I called as I walked away.

bash

HEADING out of the science building, I had my eyes on my phone when someone crying out caught my attention. Looking up, I spied two guys from my English class punching and kicking some lanky little dude who didn't have a chance in hell at fighting back.

Not cool.

I'd heard them in class before, and they were straight-up assholes who were always shit-talking and laughing about beating up some guy or fucking some girl. Dropping my bag on the ground, I strode forward with my fist cocked back, ready to rumble.

I clocked the sandy-haired one in the jaw, making him tumble back, and then slammed his head on the hard concert behind him. Next, I grabbed the other by the back of his shirt and threw him off. He didn't even notice his friend had stopped joining him in all the fun they were having. His blue eyes widened as I gripped him by the collar of his shirt, and my fist came down.

Sandy hair was sputtering and trying to get to his feet as I hit his friend again and again. "Wow, man," he coughed and grabbed for my arm. He was easy enough to shake off, landing on his ass. "What the hell, man? We've never done anything to you," he shouted from where he was sprawled out on the ground.

I dropped his friend and rounded on him. "Are you telling me he did something to you?" I pointed to where the guy they were beating up was still laid out on the ground and curled up in a fetal position.

"He looked at my girlfriend," he said petulantly.

"Which girlfriend is that? I hear you constantly talking about fucking different girls all the time in class. Is one more special than the other?" I looked up at the quickly darkening sky and laughed. A storm was rolling in. Soon it would darken the sky to match my mood.

"What the fuck, Darren?" A girl from the crowd shouted. I turned to see a tiny blonde come running toward who I guess was named Darren. She stood in front of him with her eyes narrowed, and then, just as quickly as she came, the blonde reared back her foot and kicked him in the balls before running off with tears threatening to spill down her cheeks.

Darren cradled his balls as he rolled around on the ground, moaning. I turned toward the other guy, and he was out cold—something I hadn't even realized.

Moving to the kid they were beating up, I helped him off the ground and made sure he was steady.

"Thanks. You didn't have to do that," he mumbled from his cracked and swollen mouth.

I didn't, but I wanted to punch someone, and those two assholes were good targets. Plus, they needed to pick on someone their own size.

I looked him up and down. He was short and so damn skinny even that guy's girlfriend could beat him up. "You need to grow a pair before someone else tries to beat you up. At least start hitting the gym and bulking up."

"I…" his mouth hung open as he stared at me.

"I won't be around to save your ass next time." I tapped him with my shoulder and stalked off through the crowd that had gathered. What a bunch of fucking losers.

I made my way through a shortcut that was barely lit by the darkening sky as I headed to my bike. Soon it would be too cold, and I'd have to put her up for the winter and would miss taking her out on the open road during the winter months. The sight of two guys loitering around by my bike in the parking lot had me immediately on edge. No one messed with my bike and lived.

I kept my helmet in my backpack. If they both came at me at the same time, I could swing my backpack and clock one of them with my helmet. It would be unexpected and give me a chance to take the other guy.

"Can I help you?" I asked as I slowly walked up to them and my bike. My eyes scanned them and surveyed my ride to make sure they hadn't done anything to her.

They were both the same height as me and a little less bulky, but I knew they could lay me out if they wanted to. Their dark eyes glinted as an overhead light came on.

"We saw what you did back there," the thinner of the two said. He had on all black with a pair of aviators clipped over the collar of his t-shirt.

"Just doing my civic duty for the day." They didn't know I didn't give one shit about that kid. If they weren't careful, I might take them on as well.

The other cocked a brow as he took a slow drag from his cigarette. "Oh, the little guy was a good cover. I like what you did there. No one would be the wiser that you stole his wallet right after you saved him from getting his ass kicked even more by those two fools."

How the hell did these two see that? I hadn't

noticed them when I was out there, and I noticed everything.

"Don't worry." He took a drag and slowly let it out. "We don't care. In fact, we thought you'd be perfect for helping us out if you want to make some extra money."

I could always use extra money. I was living in a piece of shit apartment that was cold as hell last winter, and school was eating up every penny I had.

"Ah, look at his eyes light up, and he doesn't even know what it is yet," the other one laughed.

"As long as it's not gay porn, I don't care." I sat my backpack down on the ground by my legs and crossed my arms over my chest. "What will I have to do?"

"What's wrong with gay porn?" They both said at the same time.

Were they boyfriends?

"Nothing, but I'm not interested in guys, so there's no way in hell I'm going to be fucking some guy for money."

"I've heard that before and then…" the thinner one shrugged with a smirk.

"I'll never be that desperate. No offense if you two are boyfriends or whatever."

They turned to look at each other and then started to laugh hysterically. I wasn't sure what was so funny, but whatever. Maybe they were just fucking with me and wanted me in on some threesome.

"You just made my day." The one who was smoking on a wheezy laugh. "We're brothers, and before you say anything," he held his hand up. "We don't fuck. There's no incest happening in this family."

Well, that was good to know. I didn't have an innocent mind, but it sure as hell didn't go there.

"Good to know." I lifted a brow at them. "What is your way of making money?"

They looked at each other and had a silent conversation, and then finally nodded. When they turned back to me, they had matching smirks on their faces. It was then I could see the resemblance.

"Meet us tomorrow at four o'clock at the skate park," the skinny one said.

"Do I at least get to know your names before I meet you tomorrow?"

They both shrugged at the same time, one their left shoulder and the other their right. It was weird.

"I'm Alejandro," the skinny one said. "But you can call me Ale."

Throwing down his cigarette and then stepping on it with his heel, the other one smirked. "I'm Armando."

"I'm Bash."

Matching smirks lit up their faces. "We know." I

wanted to ask them how they knew but didn't get the chance before they walked off. I had a feeling those two were trouble, and we were going to have a lot of fun.

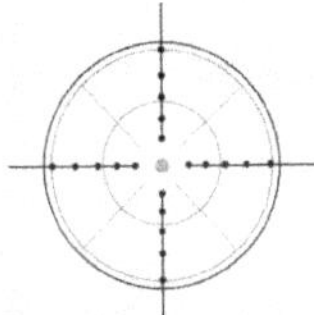

I'D BEEN DRAGGING ASS all day. I wasn't sure what it was, but I couldn't sleep last night. It didn't help that I'd run out of coffee and hadn't been to the store yet to buy more. There was no way in hell I was hitting up the local Starbucks on campus and paying five dollars for a fucking coffee. I'd rather be tired than waste my money.

Parking my bike in the parking lot, I scanned for the brothers but didn't see them. If they stood me up, I would kill them the next time I saw them.

Getting off my bike, I placed my helmet on the seat and walked out into the open park. My hands clenched at my sides as I looked around. There were plenty of people here on their skateboards, but not the brothers. Just as I was about to turn around and head back to my bike, I spotted them. There were far off to the side with their backs turned, making it hard to recognize them. One of them shook hands with someone, and then the other person walked off, shoving his hands in his pockets.

Moving around the outside of the crowd, I made my way toward the brothers but slowed my pace and observed as someone else stepped up to them. They said a few words. Alejandro slipped his hand into the pocket of his jeans and then shook hands with the guy before the interaction was over. I had a pretty good idea of what was going on here.

As if they could hear me walking, they turned as one and landed their dark eyes on me. I wasn't sure how they heard me. I was stealthy, and no one ever heard me as I approached them—no one except for that smoke show that took me by surprise in the alley. Damn, that was hot. What I wouldn't give to see her in a dark alley and have her push me up against the rough brick to have her way with me again.

There was nothing sexier than a woman who knew what she wanted.

I dug the blunt tips of my fingernails into the palm of my hand as I tried to ward myself from thoughts of that night. I didn't want to roll up on these guys with a hard-on trying to bust through my zipper. Taking a deep breath, I focused my mind on the task at hand: these two dudes and how I could make my money so I wasn't scraping by for the next couple of years.

"We weren't sure if you were going to make it," Armando said, his eyes lit up with mischief.

Was this a test? I crossed my arms over my chest as I locked down my face. I knew they wouldn't be able to read anything on my face as I spoke. They didn't need to know how desperate I was to get out of my circumstances. "Like I said before, I'm pretty much down for anything, so hit me with what you've got."

"We don't trust easily, but we saw something in you that makes us think you'll be good for the job."

I had no idea what they possibly could have seen that would make them think they could trust me. We met twenty-four hours ago, and I sure as shit didn't trust them.

"There's been an uptick in sales here at the skate park, and we're normally at school. We need someone who can take this spot." Alejandro said so matter-of-factly like they weren't selling drugs to the skaters here.

I turned to look at the crowd of people enjoying the sun and skating. It wouldn't last. Once it got cold in a couple of months, they'd be inside, and I'd be without money again.

"Starting off, we'll pay you a thousand a week. If you move more product than we think you will, we'll give you a bump." Armando shrugged like a thousand dollars was chump change to him, and it probably was.

I took them in again. I didn't know shit about designer clothes or brands, but everything they had on looked expensive. Their tennis shoes were at least a couple of hundred bucks. They could definitely afford a thousand a week, if not more.

"And what happens if I get caught?"

Alejandro's eyes narrowed into slits. "Then you don't know us."

"Never even heard of us," Armando supplied.

Got it. I was on my own.

"When do you want me to start?"

Armando's brows rose. "Have you ever sold blow before?"

"Can't say that I have, but I'm not going to try to sell it. They'll come to me if they want it."

"Exactly," they said at the same time, with identical smiles. "I think you'll do just fine. Make sure to bring a skateboard so that you look like you're part of the crowd."

I looked them up and down. They so didn't look like the skaters here. I didn't have the baggy clothes they wore, nor did I have a skateboard. Was this a test? I'd steal one of these punks' boards if I had to.

Armando looked behind me and chuckled. "We'll have a board waiting for you when you get out of class tomorrow." He handed me a piece of paper. "Once the park clears out tomorrow, meet us at this address to give us the money, and we'll give you more product."

Sounded easy. Too easy.

If this was a setup, I'd kill them when I had a chance.

Alejandro patted me on the shoulder. "Don't worry. We won't fuck you over unless you fuck us over."

I wanted to ask why me, but I didn't really care. I'd be their best seller for as long as I lasted. By this time next week, I'd be living a whole different life.

arely

1 Month Later

A SOFT KNOCK at my door has me looking up from my computer screen. Looking across the room, I noticed the time. It was almost midnight. I stretched my arms over my head as I called out. "Come in."

Ale and Army stepped into my office. They were laughing like they always did when they were together. They had at least a thousand inside jokes that only they understood.

"Jefa," they said at the same time.

I nodded to them and waited until they sat across from me. "Boys, how are things?"

"Good," Ale answered.

Army looked to his twin and rolled his eyes. "Better than ever with the new guy."

"That's what I like to hear. Where are you going to put him once it's winter?"

"We're not sure yet. Maybe at school," Army answered.

"When you figure it out, let me know. Not that I don't enjoy you two coming to visit me, but it's late, and I want to get home. What did you come to speak to me about?"

Army pulled out a cigarette but quickly put it away. He knew I didn't allow smoking in my office, and he also knew I didn't like his smoking. Our father had been dying of lung cancer when he met his end, and I didn't want the same fate for my baby brother.

"Why don't we walk you out and tell you what we're thinking?" Ale stood and headed for the door.

"I like that idea." I closed my laptop and put it inside my messenger bag, along with a few other papers I would need tomorrow. "Are you both coming home, or are you staying at the dorm tonight?" The night was still young for them. As much as I didn't want to think about it, my brothers were attractive and young. The fact that they were here instead of off fucking someone said they were serious about whatever it was that brought them to me.

Army held his arm out for me to take as we walked to the door. "Where's Santi?"

"He's taking care of a matter."

"He should be here with you when you're out this late at night," Army tried to argue.

I couldn't help but laugh. These boys thought I was helpless. If only they'd witnessed the attempted mugging a month ago, they wouldn't think I was so weak.

"It's his job to protect you," Ale argued.

"And what are you doing now? Are you going to let something happen to me?"

"Of course not, but what would you have done if we weren't here?"

"I would have walked out by myself like the capable woman I am. If I thought I was in any danger, I wouldn't have sent Santiago off." I gave Army's arm a little squeeze, letting him know I appreciated his concern, but none was needed. "You're wearing on my patience. Now tell me what brought you here."

Ale turned and stopped in the narrow hall. He leaned casually against the wall. "The new guy, Bash, we want to submit him for the Scorpio Society."

That brought me up short. The society wasn't easy to get into. You had to pass a test, and each test was different. It would test you in ways you never thought possible, and if you passed, you were part of a secret society that would ensure your place in the world. My father was the first in our family to be inducted. Every member of our family was a part of it, and each year a member could submit someone they thought would be valuable to the society.

I pushed Ale to keep moving. "You think he'll pass?"

"We wouldn't suggest him otherwise," Army answered for his brother.

"If he passes, he can't be a street corner dealer, you know?"

"We know," they said in unison.

"I want to meet him first. Let me get a read on him, and then if he passes the test, we'll discuss where he'll be the most useful. If the test doesn't work out, will he be missed?"

There was always the possibility you might not live through the test. Of course, he wouldn't know that. Not until it was too late.

"When we first met Bash, he was living in a shit hole apartment, but he's since moved into a nicer place. He never talks about family or friends. He's got no one."

I wanted to stop walking, but my need to get home overrode the urge. "Do you talk to him about your family?"

I could feel Army's penetrating gaze on me. He was five inches taller than me, and I hadn't worn heels today. Still, I didn't look up. "We're not stupid, jefa. He only knows about us and only surface-level shit."

"Good. Bring him by the house tomorrow afternoon." We stepped out of the hall and into the back portion of the church. Taking a moment, we each did the sign of the cross before leaving out the back way that only we used.

Silently, we walked to my car. Ale opened the door for me and waited. Leaning up, I kissed Army's cheek and then moved to Ale. I gave him a kiss too before I got inside my car and turned it on. "Go enjoy the rest of your night."

Ale leaned inside and smirked. "You should have more fun in your life, Arely."

"That's not easy to do when you're running the biggest syndicate on the eastern seaboard." Who had time for fun when there was money to be made and hundreds of people to watch over?

"Still, you should find someone who makes it worth the time away from ruling the world."

Oh, to be so young and naïve. If only it was that easy.

I blew them a kiss. "I'll see you tomorrow."

They both saluted me and walked off into the shadows before I drove off.

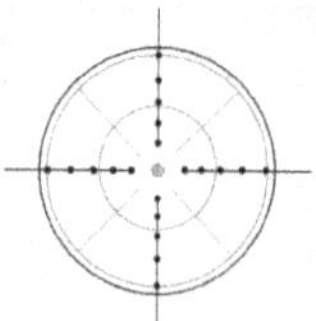

I WAS FINISHING up my late lunch when my phone pinged with an alert, letting me know Alejandro and Armando were here with their guest.

Ale was the first in the kitchen. He greeted me with a kiss on the cheek and then went to the fridge for something to eat. It was almost impossible to keep the fridge stocked with five men living in the house. Luckily for me, they didn't like most of the food I ate, so they left it alone. Santi, on the other hand, was constantly complaining about how someone had eaten something of his.

Army was laughing when he stepped into the kitchen. There was a deep, sexy chuckle that followed that I knew didn't belong to my brother, and it had me curious about their new friend. I wasn't prepared for who walked in with Army. Even though it had been dark, I would have been able to identify the man who tried to mug me anywhere. Immediately, I was on edge. Was he here to fuck with us? What were the odds he'd try to steal my purse, and then my brothers would find him?

"Jefa, this is Bash. He's the one we've been telling you about," Army introduced him.

Maybe I should have asked to see a picture of him before they brought him, but never in my wildest dreams did I think it would be *him*.

Bash stopped dead in his tracks as he took me in. Yeah, he remembered me too. It was an encounter I would never forget, and I bet he wouldn't either.

I stood from my seat at the table and moved to stand in front of it. I squared my shoulders as I took him in. He had on all black, and his hair had grown out a little more on top. The sides were cropped close and a dark brown, while the top was turning shaggy and a light to medium brown. His light brown eyes were laser-focused on me. Damn, they were a gorgeous color. They drew me in without me wanting them to. The skateboard he was holding in his left hand dropped to the floor, snapping me out of my perusal.

"What's your full name?" I demanded. I was going to have Santi do a background check on him immediately.

"Sebastian King," he answered without hesitation. The deep timbre of his voice sent a tingle down my spine. Why was he having this effect on me?

"Leave me alone with him," I ordered.

Ale and Army didn't hesitate to do what I asked of them. Ale looked back at me with his brows pulled together before they disappeared out of the kitchen, leaving Sebastian and me alone.

Sitting on the edge of the table, I crossed my arms over my chest. It didn't escape my notice how Sebastian's nostrils flared as his eyes were drawn to my full breasts that were pushed up with the movement. "Did you know who I was when you tried to rob me?"

"I don't know who you are now except Alejandro and Armando's sister. Did you send them for me? Have they been playing me?"

I threw my head back and laughed. "They have no idea we've met before today."

A sexy smirk spread across his chiseled face. "Are you going to tell them?"

"I don't share who I fuck with my brothers. If you want to inform them, go right on ahead." He'd be lucky they didn't kick his ass when they found out. "My brothers say you're good. Are you done trying to steal from poor defenseless ladies?"

Sebastian moved further into the kitchen, leaving

only a few feet of space between us. "I would say you were far from defenseless."

True, but he didn't know that when he tried to rip me off.

Pushing away from the table, I walked toward Sebastian. There may have been a little extra sway in my step. I couldn't help it. There was something about him that called to me. If my brothers weren't waiting for us, I'd climb him like I did in the alleyway and have my way with him. Running the tip of my black fingernail along his jaw, I put on my best don't fuck with me smile. "If you're going to work for us, there are some ground rules, and the first one is you don't steal from women."

"Is this because I tried with you?"

Stopping the perusal of his face, I dug my fingernail into the cleft of his chin. "Unless you're given orders, leave women alone. It's plain and simple. I don't care who you go after as long as they're male and not in my family."

Dipping his head down, making my nail dig further into his chin, Sebastian smiled like he wasn't phased in the least. "I knew you were one badass motherfucker that night, but I had no idea just how much." His left hand ran up from my hip to my ribs and then rubbed his thumb over the swell of my breast. This boy was cocky, and if he had been any other man, I would have chopped off his hand for daring to touch me without permission. "You run all of this?"

My back stiffened. "I do. Do you have a problem with a woman in charge?"

"Oh, mami, you should know by my performance the other night I have zero problems with a woman taking charge. In fact, I wouldn't mind running into you again. Maybe we can replay our night in the alley."

"Do you fuck many people in alleys?" I snapped. I went the next day to get tested, which, luckily for him, came back negative.

His thumb brushed over my oversensitive nipple as he smirked down at me. "I can say you're my one and only. How about you? Do you regularly fuck men who try to attack you?"

"I can say you're my first as well." I pulled out of his hold and pushed by him. "We should find Ale and Army before they wonder if I've killed you and fed you to the pigs."

"Do you really have pigs here?"

Looking over my shoulder, I looked him up and down, more than liking what I saw. He moved like a jungle cat and had the aura of a man in charge. Even with that presence about him, I somehow knew he wouldn't fuck us over. "I wouldn't do anything to find out."

We found Army and Ale outside arguing by the pool. The second they saw me, they froze and waited for a sign on whether I thought Sebastian would be a good fit for the society. I didn't know anything about Sebastian aside from what they'd told me, and while I'd hate it if, by some chance, he didn't pass, I thought he'd make an excellent addition to the society.

I gave them a nod, showing my stance on the matter—one Sebastian didn't have any knowledge of.

Santi appeared in the doorway with Pablo next to him. From the firm set to their mouths, I knew whatever they had to say wasn't going to be good.

"Hermana, we've got a problem," Santi grumbled, his eyes darting toward Sebastian. He wasn't sure whether to say more in present company.

"We've got a problem with one of the trucks," Pablo added.

My job was never done.

"It was nice to meet you finally, Sebastian."

"Call me Bash," he offered. I liked calling him by his full first name when everyone else didn't.

My gaze went to my brothers, who were back to arguing. "I expect to see you at Sunday dinner."

"Of course." They moved in sync toward me and kissed me on my cheeks. "Sunday."

They motioned for Sebastian to follow after them.

Being his own man, Sebastian took my hand in his and brushed his lips against the skin below my knuckles, sending a jolt of electricity straight to my clit. He looked up at me with his long eyelashes fanning out over his cheeks, and those light brown eyes told me he knew exactly what his touch was doing to me. "I hope to see you again soon."

I wouldn't mind seeing him either, but I didn't utter those words aloud. Instead, I gave him a tight-lipped smile before I took my hand back. Then I sauntered into the house, following behind Santi and Pablo, readying myself to put out another fire.

bash

FOR THE LAST WEEK, I couldn't get her out of my head. She was in my every thought, and I didn't even know her damn name. It was a slow day at the skate park since it was getting colder, so I decided today would be perfect for dropping by to see her.

Twenty minutes later, I pulled up on my bike to the gates that surrounded the house. A big burly guy stepped out of the shadows before I had a chance to even hit the intercom.

"Do you have an appointment?" He asked in a heavy Spanish accent.

I was sure he knew I didn't. He probably knew of every appointment that occurred.

"I don't, but I want to see the boss. Tell her Ba…

Sebastian is here to see her." Once she knew I was here, she'd let me through.

The big guy took two steps back, hit a button on the earpiece I now saw he was wearing, and spoke quietly. This was some next-level shit here. My eyes darted around to what I could see with the ten-foot-high stone security wall. There were cameras and bound to be more security guards on the premises. It wasn't until then that I grasped the full extent of who she, Alejandro, and Armando were. They weren't a small-time operation. They were the top dogs, and somehow, they saw something in me and brought me in.

Two seconds later, he stepped back up to me and my bike. His brows were pulled tight, and he looked pissed. I had a feeling he didn't like my unannounced arrival.

I'd barely pulled up to the house before a man who had to be Ale and Army's brother came out. He was tall with dark hair and the same dark eyes they all shared. He looked like one I saw the other day when I was here. If I thought the security guard was unhappy to see me, this guy was pissed. His steps were fast as he rounded up on me and pulled a gun to hold to my temple out of nowhere.

"What gave you the dumb fucking idea you could just show up here out of the blue?" He growled out.

"Santi," she said in a bored tone. "Leave him be. He doesn't know the rules."

"Well, maybe someone needs to teach him." A nasty smirk grew on his face. "I'll happily take him out back and make sure he knows good and well what we expect out of this little bitch boy."

Bitch boy?

I reared up on him, using the two inches of height I had over him to look down at this asshole. "You might want to think twice about calling me a little bitch boy."

"Let me shoot him, A. He's a dime a dozen."

"He's already been tapped to take the test." Her voice grew closer until she had her hand on his shoulder and pushed him away. I got my first look at her in the sunlight. The sun glinted off her black hair, almost making it look dark blue. Her big brown eyes narrowed as she looked at her brother. Her plush lips were ruby red. What I wouldn't give to have them around my cock, leaving red streaks that I knew I wouldn't want to wash off for days. "Leave him. He'll either be in soon or no more."

What the hell did that mean? What test? No one told me about a test. If I didn't pass, I wouldn't work for them any longer?

This Santi fellow looked me up and down, and he found me wanting. He thought I was useless, and I didn't blame him. I was tricked out to look like a loser stoner skater boy. Little did he know I was far from the boy I looked *and* I'd fucked his sister in a seedy alleyway.

Or maybe he did know, and that's why he hated me.

"Come," she gripped me by the wrist and started to pull me away from her brother. I followed and looked over my shoulder at him with a big shit-eating grin before I mouthed, fuck you. "Stop antagonizing him. He will shoot you and won't think twice about it."

How the hell did she know what I was doing? Probably the same way she knew I was behind her the night I tried for her purse.

My eyes were trained on her tight as fuck ass encased in a pair of those tight legging, yoga pant things that had my mouth watering. "So, I guess you don't get many unexpected visitors here."

"Unexpected visitors don't get warm greetings. Ever. Normally they end up dead." She said it so matter-of-factly that I was shocked she was admitting to killing people.

"What's your name?" I needed a name to put with that ass and gorgeous face.

"Is that what you came here to ask?" She looked over her shoulder at me, her red lips curled up at the ends.

"Is there something wrong with knowing your name? Is it a secret, and if I learn it, I'll have to be killed?"

She rolled her eyes and then turned back around, pulling me further into the house. There was a loud slam and then the sound of glass breaking. I heard her sigh before she spoke. "You shouldn't have antagonized him. If you live, it's going to take forever for him to like you."

What was this talk about me dying?

Instead of asking that important question, another one came out. "Does that mean you like me?"

"If I didn't like you, you'd be splattered out on the driveway right now. Like I said, we don't take kindly to unanticipated guests."

Good to know. I guess I wouldn't be dropping by unannounced anymore. Not if I wanted to keep my head.

She pulled me into a sleek office done in all black leather with gold accents and dropped my wrist. She moved to sit on the edge of her desk and lifted a brow. "Why are you here, Sebastian?"

Did I tell her the truth?

Moving until there were only inches between us, I lifted a strand of her black hair and wrapped it around my finger. "I can't stop thinking about that night in the alley. Tell me you're the same."

"You came here to get your ego stroked?" She threw her head back and cackled. "This is the wrong place for that."

So, I was seeing.

I looked at the pristine desk she was sitting on and pushed forward until the tent in my pants pressed to her front. "Have you ever fucked anyone on this desk?"

Tilting back her head, her dark eyes turned black as she licked her ruby red lips. "Ah, now I see why you really came. You want a taste of what you had back in the alley. Haven't you ever heard it's not smart to mix business with pleasure?"

"That's for people who are afraid of what they're feeling. We aren't those people." I cupped the side of her neck and looked down to find her chest was rising rapidly. "Do I scare you?"

"Not in the least." She tried to shake her head, but my hold was unrelenting. "If anyone should be afraid here, it's you."

"Tell me your name," I demanded.

"And if I do, what do I get?" She widened her legs,

giving me the perfect opportunity to step between them.

"Anything you want." My fingers dipped into the yoga pants to find her bare wet heat greeting me. "I need a name to moan when I come. Don't deny me." Gripping the sides of her pants, I pulled them down her toned legs and threw them across the room.

Dropping to my knees, I came face to face with her sweet pussy. It was already glistening and smelled so damn divine. Leaning forward, I swiped my tongue through her folds and moaned. "Tell me your name."

Her fingers tangled in my hair and pushed my head back down, not answering me. Giving her what she wanted, I feasted on her cunt. I sucked on her lips, fucked her with my tongue and fingers until she was a quivering mess. All the while, my dick was hard as stone in my pants, begging for release.

Gripping her by the hips, I angled her, laving her with my tongue in slow strokes, swirling the tip of my tongue around her hood and sucking on her swollen clit. When she was close to the edge, I pulled back and stared up at her.

"What are you doing?" She tried to push her pussy into my face, but I had a firm grip on her hips. I wasn't giving her what she wanted until I got what I came for. When she figured out I wasn't going to continue to fuck her with my tongue, she huffed and ran her hand down her stomach and over her slick center.

Grabbing her hand in mine, I shook my head. "I'm not letting you come until you tell me your name."

"You know I could just kill you for holding back on me," she growled like a kitten.

"But you won't because you like the way I fuck you, and this is only the appetizer."

She looked up at the ceiling, her chest heaving, and muttered a few words in Spanish. I had no idea what they were since I didn't speak Spanish, but I was seeing it might come in useful with this family. She blew out a loud breath through her nose and looked back down at me. "Don't make me regret this."

I waited on bated breath. What if she had a horrible name she was embarrassed about? I'd have to pretend it was a great name and then eat the fuck out of her.

"Arely," she huffed.

It wasn't a name I'd heard before, but damn, did it suit her. It was as unique as the woman with her legs spread for me.

Slipping my tongue into her slick heat, I fucked her as I rubbed my thumb in slow circles on her clit. "You taste fucking amazing, Arely," I moaned against her core and felt her shiver.

Her small hands pressed into the back of my head, letting me know she wanted more. Coating my finger with her juices, I pushed through the tight ring of her asshole until she relaxed and let me in. I couldn't wait to stick my dick where my fingers were, but that would have to wait. First, I needed inside her pussy, and then I'd take her ass.

One of her hands moved to my shoulder, where she dug her fingernails into my flesh. Her hips rocked up, chasing her release as she moaned and writhed underneath me. Damn, she was so fucking hot. I lapped at her, and when I felt her walls start to quake around my fingers, I took her bud into my mouth, sucking hard.

Arely let out a shout that rang through the room as she clenched her legs around my head and fell apart. I kept licking as I watched her back arch as another wave of pleasure shot through her. When I finally dragged every ounce of ecstasy out of her, I stood and licked my lips.

"You're astounding when you come," I told her as I pressed the heel of my hand against my raging hard-on.

Arely's eyes fluttered open, and she smiled at me. It was almost innocent, not her usual smirk or one that held malice in it.

"I want to roll you over and fuck you from behind."

"What are you waiting for? Stick that big cock of yours in me and show me what I've been missing."

She didn't have to tell me twice. I had all of my clothes off faster than she could turn over.

I slid inside with no resistance. She was so hot, tight, and slick. After listening to Arely moan for the last ten minutes, and how fucking perfect she felt, I wasn't sure how long I'd last.

She reared back and ground herself on my cock. "Don't go easy on me."

Pulling back until only my tip was inside, I slammed back inside. I fucked her hard, loving the sounds coming out of her mouth and the way she asked for more. With each hard thrust, she ground back on me, taking me even deeper. The sounds of our hips slapping together was so fucking hot.

"I need you to come," I said hoarsely. I was so damn close, but I needed to feel her walls milk my cock before I let go.

"I'm close," she panted. "I n—"

Before she could say anything, I snaked my right hand around her side and started to rub fast circles over her clit. Arely bucked up into me as her walls started to squeeze my cock like a vice. If I wasn't before, I was now utterly addicted to her pussy.

Slamming into her one last time, I gripped her hair and pulled her back to my front as I unloaded into her. I bit down on her shoulder and moaned her name.

Picking her up, I carried Arely over to the leather couch that sat in front of a row of windows. Her office looked out onto a lake with bright green grass leading down to the bank, even as the leaves were starting to change.

Sitting down, I placed her in my lap and stared out into the expanse of her estate while I ran my hands over her bare legs and ass. We were quiet for a long time. I had no idea what she was thinking, but I was thinking about how I'd put up with her brother threatening to kill me if I got to fuck her like this.

After a few minutes, I felt a warm liquid run down my leg and onto the couch. I swiped to see what the hell it could have been, only for the substance to come back white. It was then I remembered I hadn't fucked her with a condom.

I shifted to wrap my arms around her and cleared my throat. "Not to kill the afterglow of the moment, but we didn't use protection."

Pushing up, Arely stood and tapped my cheek. "You don't have anything to worry about. My father had me sterilized when I was fourteen, afraid that I'd be raped and get pregnant." Without another word, she turned and moved toward a door on the left of the room and slipped inside.

I blinked, shocked, wanting to pull her back against me.

What kind of world had I condemned myself to?

arely

THERE WAS a soft tap on my door before Santi walked inside my sanctuary. He took one look at me and halted in his steps.

"Where the fuck is Pablo?" I growled out as I looked at the spreadsheet. The numbers were chaos, and I had no idea what was wrong with them. That's why I had Pablo. He was my left-hand man. He handled the numbers, but he'd been MIA all fucking day. Santi was my right-hand man. He was my bodyguard and my best friend.

"He's doing work for the society today. I thought he told you." He eyed me up and down before he sat across from me.

"*He* didn't tell me shit, and I'm sitting here looking

at this fucking spreadsheet, *his* spreadsheet, and can't make any sense of it. Something's off, but I don't know what."

This was what I got for not handling it myself and doing it the way I wanted, but there was only so much time in the day, and I couldn't do everything.

Santi got up and came around my desk to look at the spreadsheet and then threw his hands up in the air. "I have no fucking clue what I'm looking at. It gives me a headache just trying to figure it out."

I felt the same way.

Closing my laptop, I swiveled my chair to look at my best friend. "Do you know when Ale and Army's friend has his test?"

He cocked his head and then shook it. "You know I don't. Why the interest?"

"He's making us money, and if he ends up dead, we'll have to find someone to replace him. There's only so much the twins can do while actually attending college."

Santi rolled his eyes and moved to sit back in the seat he'd vacated. "Yes, they might have to stop partying and fucking all the time."

There was a bite in Santi's words that had me wondering if he was jealous of them. We never had the chance to go to college. Instead, we were thrust headfirst into our roles when our father died, and before that, we did whatever our father instructed us to do.

"Don't look at me like that. I don't give a shit what they do, but you baby them too much. Hell, they probably don't even do their own homework and pay some chick or some nerd so they can make good grades."

Santi was probably right. If the twins could find a way out of doing their work, they would. It was safe to assume they hadn't done their own homework in years.

Leaning forward with his elbows on his knees, Santi raised one lone brow. "Are you ready to get out of here? I have plans for tonight that I'd rather not have to cancel."

Letting out a frustrated sigh, I opened my laptop back up. "You go on ahead. I have some more work I need to do, but I'd hate for you to miss out on your date."

"It's not a date," he shot back so fast I knew it was exactly that.

"You know you're free to have a love life. Don't let me or work stop you."

"The same thing goes for you. All you do is work.

You're either here or at the house with only family around. You should get out and do something with Bree or go to a book club or something."

I threw my head back and laughed. "Oh my god, can you imagine me at a book club? First, I don't want to read their boring-ass books, and second… just no. Eventually, I'll find my thing, and until then, I'm happy with you by my side."

"Now you're making me feel bad for leaving you here. Do you want me to send one of the guards here to watch over you and escort you to your car?"

"I'm perfectly capable on my own. No one knows about this place, and if they try to take me on the road, I'll sideswipe them."

"Damn, sis, you're hardcore," he laughed, but he knew it was true.

Dismissing him with a shoo of my hand, I settled into my chair, preparing for a long night. "Go and have fun for me."

He stood and came around to kiss me on the cheek. "Text me when you're leaving and when you get home, so I know you're good."

"I will. Now get out of here."

I watched as he left and got back to work. It was two hours later when I was finally done and ready to go home. My eyes were bleary from looking at my computer screen for so long as I texted Santi that I was leaving and slipped out into the cool night. Pulling my hood over my head, I hunkered down in my jacket as the cold air hit my skin. The heel of my boot got stuck in a crack of one of the cobblestones, irritating the fuck out of me. I bent down to dislodge my heel when I heard someone coming up behind me.

I whirled around to see Sebastian coming at me with a knife in his hand.

"What the fuck?" I gasped as I fell on my ass and started to rip off my boot.

The second Sebastian saw me, he ran to my side, and bent down to help.

I pushed him away and stood with only one boot on. "What are you doing here?"

"Some test. What are you doing here?" He looked around the area as if he was looking for someone else.

"It doesn't matter why I'm here. What's your test?" I hissed as I took an uneven step back.

"There was supposed to be someone coming out of the church with a hood on. When I saw the person, I was supposed to kill whoever it was. That's some fucked up test. Did you do this?"

"I didn't have to kill anyone, but yes, I took the

test." I looked over my shoulder at the church, knowing I was the only person here, and I was most likely the target since I always put my hood up when I wore my coat. "I think you were sent to kill me."

Sebastian's knife fell to the ground, and a second later, a shot rang out.

bash

THROWING MYSELF OVER ARELY, I tried to look over my shoulder to see where the threat was but couldn't see anything. This damn church's security was shit. There was one lone light at the side exit Arely came out of. Whoever sent me to kill her knew I wouldn't be seen, and neither would they.

My arms tightened around her thin frame and hugged her to me even more. Leaning in, I spoke so only she could hear me. "Are you okay?" I waited for a long moment, and when Arely didn't answer, I knew something was wrong. She couldn't be in shock. Hell, the woman attacked me when I tried to rob her. She was calm when I told her I was sent to kill someone.

Her.

Pulling back, I laid her on the ground and turned her over. There was a big red spot that was growing by the second, sweeping through the white material on her abdomen. Her usually sparkling eyes were closed, and her body was lifeless on the cold, wet ground.

"Arely," I rushed out as I put one hand over the blood and pressed down. Using my other hand, I placed two fingers at the pulse point on her neck and prayed to a God I didn't believe in for her to be alive. She had a pulse, but it was weak.

What the fuck do I do now?

Her warm blood coated my hand as I tried to stop the bleeding, snapping me out of my freak out. I needed to call an ambulance before whoever ordered this hit was successful and then killed me as well.

Pulling out my phone with a shaking hand, I unlocked it and quickly dialed 911.

"911, what's your emergency?" A male voice answered.

"My…" Fuck, what was Arely to me? I couldn't say boss, and she wasn't my friend. There was no category for us. "My girlfriend's been shot. We're at a church." For a brief second, my mind seized as I tried to remember the address that had been in the envelope I'd received only two hours ago. It was amazing how much your life could change in such a short period of time.

I rattled off the address and hung up. Sitting down on the ground, I ripped my off hoodie, pulled Arely into my arms, and pressed the sweatshirt to her wound, all the while trying to keep an eye on our dark surroundings. What if whoever shot her was still out there?

As I put more pressure on the wound, she moaned in pain. Even though the sound was agonizing to hear, I was just happy to know she was still alive.

"Arely, stay with me. I called an ambulance, and it should be here soon. Don't give up on me," I demanded.

Even in the dark, I could see she was pale, probably from all the blood loss. Her big brown eyes fluttered open, and I swear my heart nearly stopped as I watched a lone tear streak down her cheek.

"It's going to be okay." I tried to reassure her. "Help will be here any second."

I think she tried to nod her head, but she wasn't quite successful. Instead, it only listed over to the side until her face was flush with my naked chest.

"Seb…" her words stopped as her eyes slowly started to close once more.

"No, no, no." I shook her in my arms until, with heavy lids, she eventually opened her eyes enough to look at me. "You are not dying on me. This is not how our story is going to end."

Her mouth opened and closed a few times before she managed to get out one word. "Danger."

My gaze tracked up to scan our surrounding area. "I know. I'm keeping a lookout." There was a noise to our right, but it was so dark I couldn't see anything. Arely's tiny, cold fingertips skated along my neck, making me look down.

"Don't let them get me," she said shakily.

"I promise you I will never let anything happen to you. Not now. Not ever," I vowed. I'd never meant anything more in my life. I knew from that moment on I would give my life for Arely without thinking twice about it.

In the distance, the sound of sirens started to fill the otherwise quiet night. I crushed Arely to me, only for her body to feel lifeless in my arms.

"Arely," I shook her, watching as her arm fell to the side and her hand slapped the ground. Laying her back on the ground, I tried to feel for her pulse, only for nothing to be there.

My heart skipped a beat as I moved my fingers around, desperate to be wrong.

I had no idea what I was doing as I placed my

hands over her chest and started to pump. I wasn't sure if I was even doing it right. My only knowledge was from movies and television shows. Dipping down, I blew two puffs of air into her mouth and started to go back to pumping her chest when I was gripped by the shoulder.

The night had gone deathly silent once I started my attempt at CPR, my heavy breaths the only sound as I tried to bring Arely back. I hadn't heard the ambulance pull up or anyone get out. My sole concentration was on the beautiful but lifeless woman laid out in front of me.

"We'll take it from here, sir," one of the EMTs said. I had no idea which one. I could only sit there and watch as they worked on Arely for a minute before loading her up on the stretcher and placing her in the ambulance. They asked me questions, but I didn't remember what they were or if I even answered them. All I remembered was sitting beside her holding her hand, when the monitors started to shriek, and one of the EMTs shouted, "Flatline!"

I sat in a daze as I watched the EMT work on Arely. Sticking in an IV and pushing medicine as I gripped her hand even harder, wishing I could give all of my strength to her—except life didn't work that way.

They worked on her until we got to the hospital, only for her to be whisked away and I never saw her again.

END OF PART OF ANTHOLOGY.

Want more of King's Vow with Arely and Bash? Pre-order the full novel now. Coming this November.

arely

WHY DID EVERYTHING HURT?

I tried to open my eyes to no avail.

Why was there water dripping on my hand?

I tried to pull my hand away, only for it to be grabbed up and pressed against something prickly. My fingers jerked. I knew they did.

"Arely," came from Santi's strained voice. "Open your eyes for me. Please," he begged.

Where was I, how did I get here, and why did Santi sound devastated?

Flashes of leaving the sanctuary and finding Sebastian outside with a knife in his hand flitted through my consciousness. Then the pain, being in Sebastian's arms and him vowing to always keep me safe, and then nothing. I couldn't remember anything after that.

Where was Sebastian?

Was he okay?

Did he get shot?

"Arely, come back to us," Santi demanded in a quiet whisper.

I was trying. I really was. It was so hard to break free from the fog that pulled my limbs down into the thick muck and made my eyelids feel like they were caked in concrete.

"I felt her hand twitch. I know she's going to open her eyes any minute now." Santi's voice cracked as it filled with desperation.

"I think you're imagining things," Pablo said from a distance. "She's been unconscious for three days now."

Three days?

I struggled to open my eyes and my mouth to speak to them. I needed to get up and tell Santi I was fine.

"I saw her finger move," Army said from my other side. "We really need to get her out of here before whoever tried to kill her tries again."

He was right. If someone in the society wanted me dead, I wasn't safe unless I was at home.

"There are two guards posted just outside, and the

four of us in here. She safe for the time being," Santi argued.

I knew nothing bad could ever happen to me with my brothers by my side.

"How can you say that? I mean, where the hell were you, Santi? You're her bodyguard, and for some reason, you weren't there with her. Maybe you want her dead so you can take over."

My hand was dropped, and there was a scuffle and bang. If I could have rolled my eyes at them, I would have. I would have yelled at them as well if my mouth was working. They were fighting when they should have been trying to figure out who wanted me dead.

I kept shouting in my head for them to stop until, eventually, the word passed my lips. It wasn't a yell. It was barely more than a scratchy whisper coming up my dry, abused throat.

"Holy shit, Arely," Santi croaked. My eyes cracked open just in time to see him skid across the cheap linoleum floor of the hospital room. Wrapping his arms around me, he hugged me, burying his face in my neck. "Don't ever do that to me again. I thought we were going to lose you."

Everyone crowded around my bed, touching some part of me, and it made me truly grateful for my family and their love. I couldn't imagine being in their shoes.

If any of them had been shot, I would have been so fucking worried and then burned the world down to find out who did it and end them with a slow and torturous death.

Turning his head, Santi whispered into my shoulder. "You took twenty years off my life."

I rested the side of my head against his. "I know. I'm sorry. When can I get out of here?" Every word that came out of my mouth felt like I was swallowing glass. It must have sounded like it since Santi stood and moved to pour me a glass of water.

Ale laughed. "Of course, you'd want to know when you can get out. You've been awake for all of five seconds, and you're ready to book. You died, Arely. Fucking died. If it weren't for Bash doing CPR on you, we'd be having your funeral right now."

I took a few long swallows of the water I was given and let it soothe the burn that trailed down my throat. Only then did I speak again. It didn't hurt quite as much this time around when I spoke. "Where's Sebastian?"

All of a sudden, no one would look at me. I tried to sit up to catch their eyes until a shooting pain rocked me from the inside out. I clutched my side and clenched my teeth together to prevent from screaming.

"Fuck, A. What are you doing? You're going to rip

your stitches." Army pushed me down and kept a hand on my shoulder to keep me from sitting up. It wouldn't be hard. As much as I hated to admit it at that moment, I was weak.

Reaching up to grip Armando's hand, I dug my fingernails into the back of it, letting him know I meant business. "I'm trying to get an answer out of one of you fuckers. Where the fuck is Sebastian?" I growled out.

"In the basement. We weren't sure if you'd want to talk to him before we ended him or not."

"What the fuck?" I shouted. "Why would he be in the basement? You just said he saved my life."

"He could be lying," Pablo spoke up from the end of the bed. "We can't take any chances with your safety."

"It wasn't Sebastian who shot me. While I don't know who did, I know it wasn't him. He was right by my side when we heard the shot. You need to let him go."

"I don't think that's wise. What if he had an accomplice, and being next to you is his alibi?" Pablo tried again.

"I'm the one in charge here, so what I say goes, and I am telling you right here and now that Sebastian had nothing to do with it. The second he saw it was me he was supposed to kill, he dropped his knife." I didn't remember much, but I did remember he was upset and held me close to his body. No one did that to the person they were trying to kill.

Santiago's head was giving a slight shake when he spoke. "Who the fuck did you piss off enough in the society that they want you dead?"

"No one. You know I don't have time for their shit. It would make more sense if it were someone wanting to take us out to take over our business."

"Isn't that the truth. We've been lucky so far," Ale muttered.

"You can't leave her alone ever again," Army said to Santi. "If you have something you have to do, either you call one of us or use one of the compound guards."

"Maybe we should hire more. Santi isn't enough if there's a whole brigade coming after her." Ale's face contorted as he looked down at me. "Really, A, you're lucky they were able to bring you back."

I knew I was lucky, and I might not be again if I was by myself the next time it happened—because it would happen again, especially if the society wanted me dead. I needed to figure out who was behind the attempt on my life and wipe them from the picture.

Pablo patted my foot and started for the door. "I'm going to get the doctor, so he can check you out and give you some sort of an idea of when you can break out of here."

The second he was gone, I turned to my other brothers. "When I get out of here, Sebastian better be at his house safe and sound. If not, heads are going to roll."

Santi lifted his hands in the air and took a step back. "Alright, it wasn't my idea to begin with. It was Pablo's."

"Right now, I don't care whose idea it was." I tried to sit up higher in the bed, but it hurt too damn much. Alejandro handed me a remote attached to the bed that would help. "Sebastian doesn't deserve to be locked up for saving me."

Sitting down in one of the chairs lined up by my bed, Armando nodded. "I agree, but we wanted to be sure on the off chance. Seriously, you have no idea how scared we all were. We thought we were going to lose you."

"Enough talk about me dying. I'm here now, and that's all that matters. I need one of you to go back to the house and get me a change of clothes and my toothbrush." My mouth had a horrid taste in it that the water I kept sipping on wasn't washing away.

"We'll go," Ale said with a bittersweet smile crossing his face. "We'll also let Bash out."

"Thank you. If you've been here while I was unconscious, who's been working?"

"Does your brain ever turn off?" Army chuckled.

"It's a twenty-five/eight job." They all scrunched their brows together as they stared at me. "Meaning it never ends. I need twenty-five hours in a day and eight days a week to get everything done."

Santi reached out and cupped my leg with his palm. "I can take on more. Or Pablo. No one even knows what he does with all of his time."

"Just thinking about all the work that I'm behind on is making me itch, so I just might take you up on that."

"You can't keep going like you have. If you hadn't been working so late—"

"Let's not start making this a habit," I interrupted him. "I know I should have gone home when Santi left, and I didn't. That's on me, but let's not forget someone made killing me Sebastian's test. It wouldn't have happened otherwise."

"I'm going to string whoever did this to you up by their balls and then flay his skin off inch by inch. And only then will the true torture begin," Santi growled out.

At the same time, Pablo and a gray-haired man, who I assumed was my doctor, walked in. His steps faltered as his light blue eyes widened in horror as

Pablo clapped his hand on the doctor's shoulder. He cleared his throat and made his way over to my bedside.

"Good to see you awake, Ms. Guerrera. Your brother informed me that you'd like to go home, but first I need to check you over, and then we can speak about your discharge."

If he knew what was good for him, he'd release me the minute he was done. Otherwise, I would make his life and everyone else's here as miserable as possible.

bash

I GROUND my teeth together as I heard a noise coming my way. I was in a motherfucking dungeon in Ardy's basement. I'd been stuck sitting in a chair for… I don't know how long. All I knew was it had been multiple days. No food or bathroom breaks were the thanks I got for saving their sister. At least they'd left me a few bottles of water to drink.

The door swung open, and the one brother I didn't really know stepped inside. I think his name was Pablo. He sniffed the air as his face morphed into an ugly smirk.

"You're fucking disgusting," he snarled out as he took in the water bottles scattered on the floor.

"Would you have preferred I piss myself?" I raised a brow, taunting him.

Ale and Army barged into the room and pushed Pablo to the side. "Holy hell, Pablo. What were you thinking? He's not a motherfucking prisoner. Give me the key," Ale demanded as he came to my side and picked up my cuffed arm. Kneeling down, he looked me in the eye. I wasn't sure whose eyes were filled with more fire, his or mine. "I had no fucking clue. I've been at my sister's bedside this entire time."

"How is she?" I croaked out. I'd drank the last of my water hours ago. I wasn't sure what they had piping into this room, but whatever it was made my throat dry as fuck.

"She's awake and her usual self, although she's a little slower." He nodded to himself. "It might be a good thing, though. Arely needs to slow down." There was a long pregnant pause as he stared down Pablo with an outstretched hand. Pablo threw him the key and stormed out of the room. Ale quickly uncuffed my hand and then the leg shackled to a thick steel ring in the floor before he stood up and crossed his arms over his chest. "She was pissed as hell when she learned you were here." He sniffed and wrinkled his nose. "You should get cleaned up and go see her before she tears down the house."

"Follow me," Army called from the door. "I'll take you to one of the bedrooms where you can shower, and I'll find you some fresh clothes for you to change into."

I didn't care as long as I got to see Arely. I'd been thrown into this room with no explanation, but I knew that if she died, I died. They'd kill me even though I was the one who tried to protect her and performed CPR on her until the ambulance arrived. Still, they didn't care, and if I were in their shoes, I probably wouldn't either. I was sure they were rocked to their core, knowing someone tried to take out their sister.

I had planned to take the quickest shower known to man, but once the hot water started to fall over my body, I realized I was frozen down to my bones. Even under the hot spray, my body was shaking. After I thoroughly washed from head to toe twice, I stepped out into the opulent bathroom and dried off. True to Army's word, there was a pair of black sweats set out on the counter. I quickly changed into them and started to head out the door when Arely's other brother, Santiago, stopped me. His jaw tensed as he looked me over and then started to walk away. "This way," he informed me in a monotone voice.

I had a feeling Santiago didn't like me, not that I cared. They could all go fuck themselves if they thought I was going to take locking me away for days lying down.

Santiago stopped in front of a door close to Arely's office. "No matter what she says, she needs her rest."

I wasn't sure how I became the villain in this scenario. Ale and Army had approached me and then set me up for the fucking test. I was the one who didn't kill their sister and saved her instead.

Shouldering by him, I opened the door and stepped into the room. It was massive. My entire apartment could have fit inside Arely's bedroom twice over. The entire room was done in black, gold, and gray, with a few pops of red. There was a sitting area in front of large windows that looked out onto the lake and a massive fireplace that was roaring. The room was warm, making my hyper-alert body start to feel sluggish. Arely laid in a bed that had to be custom made because it was bigger than anything I'd ever seen before. Why did such a small person need such a large bed?

Propped up by a mountain of gold pillows in the middle of the bed, Arely looked tiny with her thick blankets pulled up to her chest. Her skin was so pale and drawn. As if she could feel me thinking about her, Arely's eyes slowly drifted open, and a hint of a smile tipped her lips.

"It took you long enough," she said hoarsely.

I crossed the room to stand beside her and took her

cold hand in mine. "I didn't mean to keep you waiting." How was she so cold with the fire and blankets? "How are you feeling?"

"Better now that I'm home." With her free hand, Arely tapped the space beside her. "Come sit."

My head was already shaking before I spoke. "I should let you rest."

"I'll rest just fine with you beside me. You look as tired as I feel, and if you're here with me, I know my brothers aren't harassing you or locking you up."

"Are you saying you want me to sleep… here?" This was not what I expected when I walked inside. I thought I'd get interrogated by her about what happened that night.

While I wasn't sure it was a good idea to stay, my body had other plans. I moved around the side of the bed and laid down next to Arely.

"If you don't want to, you can leave, but it would give me peace of mind." Her mouth opened, but she didn't continue to speak. She only looked me over.

"There's more to it, isn't there." It wasn't a question. I knew there was more she wasn't telling me.

She gave a little nod of her head before she turned on her side. It was a slow process, and I could tell that she was in pain, but I also knew she didn't want my help or to comment on it. Once Arely was curled up on her side, I pulled the thick comforter over her shoulders and waited. "You failed your test, and you might be in danger."

"I can protect myself, Arely. You don't need to worry about me." Was she worried one of her brothers would try to take me out? I didn't think Alejandro and Armando would do anything, but I wouldn't put it past the other two.

She tried to smile at me, but she wasn't very successful. Her eyes kept drooping as she spoke. "All the same, it would still make me feel better if you stay here until we figure out who was behind my assassination attempt."

"What about you? Are you safe? Someone out there wants you dead. Are they going to keep trying until they succeed?"

"They're not going to succeed, but yes, I do believe this won't be the only attempt." Her eyes fluttered closed, and little puffs of breath came out of her dry, cracked lips.

A fierce need to protect Arely came over me, and I would at all costs. If she wanted me by her side, then by her side, I would be. No one was going to stop me—especially not her brothers.

I was sure that not many people get to see Arely

vulnerable like this. "I promise I won't let anyone hurt you. I failed you once, but it won't happen again."

Lifting my hand, I caressed her cheek and pushed a lock of hair behind her ear before I settled in under the blankets with her and let the warmth drag me under.

arely

WE WERE HAVING a meeting in my bedroom because all the men in the Guerrera family thought I was too weak to sit at my desk or on a lame-ass couch. I was the second oldest, but I was being treated like a baby, which was annoying. Even as a child, I wasn't treated this way.

Pablo glared at Sebastian from the other side of my bed. "Why is he still here?"

I narrowed my eyes at my brother. It had been three days since I'd been home, and they were handling me with kid gloves. "Because I asked him to stay, and that's all you need to know. Why don't you stop giving him a hard time and update me on where we are with who ordered my hit?"

"You think *they're* talking? No, they're acting just as

stupefied by this as we are," Santi growled out. "If it were anyone else, I'd be taking them downstairs one by one and getting answers out of them. But instead, *they're* saying that wasn't the test they assigned."

"And you believe them?" Pablo scoffed. "Let me handle the issue. You need to be hiring more security, anyway."

Sebastian crossed his arms over his chest in the corner of the room. "If Santiago can't be by Arely's side, then I'll be there."

"And you think we trust her life in your hands? You've got to be kidding," Pablo laughed darkly. "While these two hoodlums may think they know you, you're an outsider, and we don't trust—"

"You think you can trust someone you hire to do the job?" Sebastian interrupted him. "Hire all the people you want, but I vowed to Arely that I would protect her, and I don't go back on my word." He glanced at me and then back to where Pablo and Santiago were sitting at the bottom of my bed. "If her life is in danger, she shouldn't be driving herself. You need at least a two-car caravan with multiple guards when going places."

I sat up higher in my bed sand gritted my teeth at the pain to not show them how much I was still affected. Sebastian raised a brow at me to say I wasn't fooling him, or maybe it was to see if I'd fight back at his suggestion. I did want to fight back, but he was right. As much as I wish I could, I couldn't take on multiple people at the same time. Neither could Santi nor Sebastian.

"I'm afraid he's right. They've already sent two people after me and failed. They won't make the same mistake again. Next time it could be an army, and we need to be prepared. I want everyone safeguarded. Don't go anywhere without your guns, and I want everyone here to have at least one person assigned to them at all times. It's not just me that they could be after. If they get to you, they know I'll do everything within my power to get you back."

"Fuck," Army sighed out. "We've had it too easy, but Bash is right. We can't be complicit anymore. We're going to up our game and make ourselves invincible."

We thought we were untouchable for too long, but it was clear some changes needed to be made. Hell, even my best friend Bree didn't travel alone, and she always had at least two guards with her. Her father made sure Bree was protected at all times, even while in the house.

Looking over to Santi, I knew this was eating at him. He felt as if he'd failed me, but in all actuality, I had failed them all. I thought I was invincible and nothing was ever going to hurt me when that couldn't be further from the truth. I was just as vulnerable as the next person when faced with a gun. "Maybe we should do something like the Zees do. If Bree can handle her security, I can suck it up."

"This isn't something that's going to be short-term. This is indefinite. Are you really saying you'll be fine with having guards around you all the time?"

"I don't want them in my bedroom, office, or in the sanctuary with me. They can stay outside the door, but no further unless needed." This was an order. I couldn't let my almost dying change my life entirely.

Santi moved slowly up the bed to sit beside me and put his arm around me. "Why are you being so agreeable?"

"Because as much as I hate it, we should have implemented this a long time ago." I didn't want what happened to me to happen to any of them.

"And you're okay with letting this gringo stay by your side when you don't even know him?" He said gringo like it was a bad word, and I wondered if Santi didn't like Sebastian because he knew something had happened between us.

"The man made a promise, and I believe him." I looked at my brothers' shocked faces and tried to put them at ease. "You weren't there that night, but the second Sebastian saw it was me, he put the knife down. He threw his body over mine when we heard the shot and took off his shirt to press against my wound. We were utterly alone, and if he wanted to, Sebastian could have killed me in a heartbeat. Instead, he vowed never to let anything happen to me. Whether you like it or not, Sebastian is here to stay."

Sebastian stepped forward. "Just like that night, I will promise to the rest of you that I will lay down my life for Arely."

Tilting his head to the side, Ale asked. "Why? You owe us no loyalty."

With only a few feet between him and the bed, Sebastian's gaze landed on mine. "It's hard to explain, and I don't think you'd understand unless you've been in the same situation."

There was no way to explain the crazy connection that started in the alley. If it had been anyone else, I would have shanked them and left them for dead, but instead, I had my wicked way with him without a second thought.

Santi rushed up from the bed, nearly knocking me over in his haste. He crowded Sebastian, his eyes on fire as he spoke. "If you cross us, we won't just take you down to the basement to sit for a few days. This time, you won't be leaving. I'll make sure your last days on

Earth are filled with more agony than you could ever imagine."

Looking at me over Santi's shoulder, Sebastian's light brown eyes glowed with an untold emotion. "If I fail, I fully give you permission to end my life."

bash

"WHAT ABOUT THAT ONE?" Army nudged me in the side as he tilted his head to some random girl he thought I might be interested in. I didn't even bother to look. I wasn't here to hook up. Little did they know, I was getting plenty of action behind the door of their sister's bedroom for the last month.

I took a sip of my beer before I spoke. "Why don't you stop worrying about me and find yourself a girl?"

"I want to make sure you're happy, so you'll keep protecting my sister. Seriously, you've been by her side every night for a month straight. How are you not dying to get laid? I swear if I go more than a couple of days, I feel like I'm going to explode. I'm surprised you're not sputtering out cum because you're so backed up."

Ale and I looked at each other, and the second our eyes locked, we died laughing. I'd never heard anything more ridiculous in my life.

As I started to come down, it was on the tip of my tongue to say I had been, but both Ale and Army were packing, and so were the two guards that were a couple of tables away. If they got pissed, they could easily order for me to be taken care of. It was their money paying the salaries of their new security force, not mine.

"You don't know what I do when I'm not at the compound," I laughed. I'd only spent a handful of nights at my apartment since Arely came home, and those were the only nights I'd been alone.

Ale was still laughing silently from his side of the table as Army spoke. "I swear I haven't seen you leave by yourself since my sister came home from the hospital."

I wasn't sure how Arely's family would feel if they knew I was fucking her on the regular, but I wasn't going to be the one to spill our secret. At least not without talking to her about it. Instead, I deflected. "Why don't you go find someone to hook up with before we start to see cum leaking out of your ears? I think it's already clogged up your brain."

"Fuck you." Army punched me in the arm before

walking off to the bar and flagging down a bartender.

I turned my attention to Ale, who had a wide grin on his face. "It's hard to get to my brother, but you did. He'll be looking for a way to get you back until he outdoes you twofold, so you better watch out," he chuckled.

I looked forward to Army trying.

Taking a long pull of my beer, I set it down and asked Ale, "Are you not looking for a hookup?"

"There's probably only one other gay guy in this bar, and he's with a bunch of girls." He scrunched up his nose. "It's not really my scene."

"Why'd you let Army pick this place then?"

He lifted one shoulder before he finished off his beer. "Unlike my brother, I won't explode if I don't have sex every other day."

If I didn't get to sink into Arely's tight heat every night, I felt like I was going to lose my mind. Not that I was going to share that with him. Tonight was one of those nights I'd be without her, but I had no excuse to go back to the house with them.

It wasn't like we were exclusive. I mean, we were in the sense that we weren't fucking anyone else, but it hadn't been discussed. We didn't talk much with words —only our bodies.

Ale cocked his head to the side and examined me

for a long moment. I let him see whatever he wanted to see. I had nothing to hide. I was loyal to the Guerrera family. They took me in and changed my life when I'd been struggling. It wouldn't be something I'd ever forget. "I know something's going on with you, and it's only a matter of time until I figure it out."

I smirked and signaled for the waitress. "I've got nothing to hide from you."

"If you're not looking for anyone to hook up with, we can leave soon." Ale nodded toward the bar and shook his head. "He's already found his mark for the night."

Army strode toward us with his arm slung around the waist of a tiny woman compared to his hulking frame. His smirk grew with every step he made. "I'm going to head out. You want to give this loser a ride home?" He nodded toward me.

On instinct, I was up in his face with my teeth bared. I may have been a lot of things in my life, but I was never a loser. If I had to kick his ass to prove it, I would.

Ale pushed between us, facing me, his hands on my chest, applying pressure. "Back the fuck down. You don't want to do this."

"The fuck I don't. Just because I don't want to dip my dick into some diseased skank, he's calling me a loser. You're the fucking loser if you can't control your dick," I shouted, spitting in Army's face.

"Hey," the girl cried out. "I'm not a skank."

"Oh, so just diseased then. Good luck with that one, dude." I laughed darkly. My gaze went to Ale. "I'm out."

Turning around, I pulled out my phone and ordered myself an Uber. I'd been letting Army drive me since I'd stored my bike for the winter. Now that I was making decent money, I really needed to get myself something else to drive.

I'd barely stepped through the door of my apartment when my phone lit up with a call from Arely. She was already talking by the time I hit accept. "What the fuck happened tonight with my brothers?"

I was still fuming. Before speaking, I went into the kitchen, pulled out a bottle of tequila, and poured myself a shot. When that wasn't enough, I did two more. I could hear Arely getting more pissed off by the second. I shouldn't have answered, but I had to. What if she was in trouble?

Walking back into the living room, I threw myself down on the couch and closed my eyes, letting the tequila relax me. "Your brother called me a loser for not fucking some rando tonight, is what."

Arely was so quiet I had to pull the phone away

from my ear to see if she'd hung up. After seeing she was still on the line, I put my phone on speaker, set it down on my chest, and waited. It probably wasn't smart of me to push up on Army, but I couldn't help it. No one, not even someone who wouldn't blink twice at killing me, was going to get away with putting me down.

"Did you want to fuck someone else?" were Arely's first words after the long silence.

"No, I wanted to punch your fucking brother in the face," I growled out and slammed my fist into the cushions of my leather couch.

"You want to hit him because he wanted you to have sex?"

What the fuck?

"Did you set this up? If you want me out of your bed, all you have to do is say so." Picking my phone back up, I stared at her name on my screen. "If Santiago needs to do something, you can call me. If not, I'll see you sometime next week." Hanging up, I turned off my phone, knowing if I didn't, it would keep ringing until I threw my phone across the room and broke it.

Heaving myself up, I grabbed the bottle of tequila from the kitchen as I moved down the hall to my bedroom to drink myself to sleep.

CHAPTER ELEVEN

SLAMMING MY LAPTOP CLOSED, I growled out a frustrated sigh. Tipping my head back against the headrest, I looked up at the ceiling.

"You look like you're about ready to climb the walls," Santi called as he walked into the room. I knew there was a smirk on his face, and if I saw it, I'd want to hit it.

"I need to get out of the house and back to the sanctuary."

"Anything you can do there, you can do here. It's obvious someone else knows about your office at the church, and it isn't safe."

Ducking my chin, I leveled Santi with narrowed eyes. "Even with my ten-man entourage?"

Santiago leaned against the wall with his arms

crossed over his chest. "It's four, and I thought you were fine with more security?"

"Just because I acknowledged that it's necessary doesn't mean I like it." Nor had I liked the fact that Sebastian hadn't been by the house except once in the last week. If it didn't tip off my brothers about what was going on between us, I would show up at his apartment and demand he fuck me. He was acting like... a child.

"There's another reason for why you're so damn bitchy lately. Is your period late or something?"

My body turned to ice as my insides caught on fire. With my jaw clenched, I did my best to eviscerate my brother. "You need to leave right now before I cut your balls off."

Santi's face turned white as a sheet. He knew I meant business. "Arely," he said softly. "I didn't—"

"I don't want to hear it. You're done for the day. Call Sebastian and get him in here now. Tell him I want to roll out within the hour," I ordered as I stormed out of my office and into my connected bedroom. Maybe it wasn't the smartest to have them so close together. It seemed I was always working. Well, today, I was taking the day off and getting away from my family, who had constantly been hovering since I got home from the hospital.

"What are you going to do?"

"What I'm going to do doesn't concern you. Just let security know we'll be rolling out in an hour."

With a plan formulating, I hopped into the shower and scrubbed and shaved every inch of my body. I was going to show Sebastian everything he'd been missing the last week by looking the hottest he'd ever seen. I put on my sexiest lingerie, tight black jeans, and a low-cut black shirt that would make any man drool. I put on a coat of mascara, my signature red lipstick, and pulled my long, black hair into a high ponytail. Before I set off out the door, I slipped on my sexiest and highest-heeled black boots. I looked just like I felt, a badass bitch, and no one was going to fuck with me today.

The second I stepped out of my bedroom, Santi was waiting for me in the hall. He walked along with me, talking and trying to apologize. "You know it helps keep you safe if the security team knows where you're going."

Without looking at him, I finally responded. "They will know where I'm going. I'm just not telling you." However, it wouldn't be difficult for him to find out where we were going once we were en route unless I forbade the team from telling him. The thought brought a smile to my otherwise stoic face.

What Santi said was a low blow, and I wasn't

going to forgive him that easily. It wasn't like he had no idea what our father had done to me. Santi was the one who helped pick me off the floor after I was brought home and was lying in a pool of my own blood.

"Stop worrying about where I'm going and figure out how someone found out about the sanctuary."

"The only way someone found out about the sanctuary is if someone betrayed you." Pablo's dark eyes glistened with malice as he spoke. "Don't you find it convenient Santi had something to do that night and left you alone? What was so important? Has he told you where he was?"

Pablo's words echoed in my head like a soundtrack. Santiago was my best friend, but I knew he was hiding something from me. Still, I couldn't believe my own brother would betray me.

Santi quickened his steps until he was ahead of me and then stopped, blocking my way. "Is something going on with you and Bash?"

There was no way in hell I was going to answer him when he was hiding something from me. "Is there something going on with you that *I* should know about?"

There was only the slight widening of his eyes before he shut down. If he didn't think I saw it, something more was going on with Santi. We could read each other easily after being each other's sidekicks for most of our lives.

Pausing at the front door, I grabbed my purse. "Is Sebastian here?"

"He's outside with the rest of the team waiting for you." Stepping forward, Santi wrapped his arms around me and pulled me into a hug. I stayed stiff. I wasn't going to give in. Not today. Santi knew better than anyone how much it hurt that my choice was taken away from me. I wasn't even sure if I'd ever want kids, but now there was no possible way. While I was the head of the family, it was only my brothers who could grow our family.

I pulled out of his hold and opened the door. Looking over my shoulder, I found Santi staring back at me with sad eyes. "Don't wait up."

Sebastian was leaning on one of the two SUVs that sat out front. The moment I stepped outside, he straightened and tried to look unaffected, but he wasn't fooling me. By the time I was in the back seat and buckled up, he was trying and failing to hide his massive erection in his jeans.

"Where to, Boss?" A guy who was bigger than Lou Ferrigno said in his deep timbre of a voice. I couldn't remember his name and instead called him Hulk.

"The city." I didn't care where we went, but it

would take at least an hour to get there. I was tired of Stonewall and needed to get away. "Once we get closer, I'll let you know what I'm planning."

Hulk nodded and started to drive away. I heard him relay the information to someone else who was likely in the SUV trailing behind us.

I wasn't sure what I wanted to do except to have a good meal and be surrounded by hundreds of strangers. I'd been so isolated, and all I wanted was to feel normal. Plus, after what Santi said and knowing he was hiding something from me, I couldn't look at his face another minute.

Sebastian leaned forward, resting the side of his face against the headrest in front of him, getting my attention. "Is everything okay?"

I shifted in my seat and tapped my long, black fingernails on my thigh. "Oh, have you decided to start talking to me again?"

His jaw ticked before he leaned back and gritted out. "What's there to talk about? You didn't need me. Was I supposed to stand around your house waiting to see if you might need me and forget about the rest of my responsibilities?"

Yes, in fact, that was exactly what he was supposed to do, but I wasn't going to tell him that.

"Is this about money? Do you need more?"

Unclipping his belt, Sebastian slid into my space until our foreheads were touching. His nostrils flared as he looked down at me. "I work for my money. I am not a prostitute."

Throwing my head back, I let out an unamused laugh. My lips brushed his on the way, and all I wanted to do was kiss his mouth raw, but there was no way that was going to happen with a car full of guards. "I'm not going to pay you to fuck me. You should be compensated for guarding me when Santi isn't. You asked for the role. Did you think it was a volunteer position where you'd make no money?"

"I didn't do it to make more money," he gritted out quietly.

"Then why?"

"Because I want you safe." His gaze locked with mine, and I knew he was telling me the truth. I could feel it radiating between us. "But if you'd rather have one of the new guys and keep me on the streets, I'll deal."

Reaching out between us, I hooked my pinky with his. "I only want you. Now enjoy the trip."

We kept quiet for the rest of the drive as we looked at the scenery out of our respective windows. Still, it didn't stop Sebastian from rubbing his thumb over the top of my hand and the pulse point at my wrist.

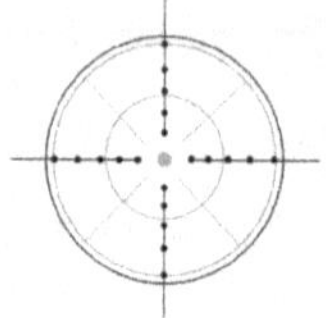

SEBASTIAN LOOKED AROUND THE TINY, dimly lit restaurant with red and white checkered cloth-covered tables scattered throughout the place. "Why here?"

"Because sometimes a girl just needs to eat her weight in carbs, and Italian is always good for that. Are you implying that just because I'm Latina, I can't eat Italian?"

Sebastian sat back in his chair and took a sip of his water. "I didn't say that, but this doesn't seem like your kind of joint."

"When I come to the city, I want the best, and this is the best damn Italian in New York City. It's run by this old Italian couple who opened this place forty years ago. What about you? What's your favorite food?"

He shrugged and looked down at the menu. "My family didn't have much money for food growing up, so I ate mac and cheese, ramen, and chicken nuggets." He looked around the room and then back at me again. "Do you think it's safe here?"

It was sweet that he was worried. "Do you think someone is going to try to take me out in the city with hundreds of people around?"

"I'm sure if a rival saw the opportunity, they'd take it. In all actuality, I'm surprised this was the first time anyone's tried to take you out."

He wasn't wrong; it was surprising. I guess I'd been lucky the last three years.

"You act like I've been running the family business since I was born. I took over after my father was killed three years ago." Even to my own ears, it sounded stupid that up until this moment, I'd had such a lack of security.

"Oh, I can see baby Arely kicking ass and taking names while running…" he tilted his head side to side as if he was afraid to say the word.

"You can say cartel," I laughed.

His light brown eyes flared. "Don't you worry?" He nodded around the room.

"You act like I shouted when I merely said the word. No one is listening to us. We wouldn't be here otherwise."

He nodded. "Do you want to tell me why we're really here in the city?"

"Because I was tired of feeling like I'm on lockdown in my own house. My brothers won't stop hovering, and they're driving me crazy."

"You know, they did almost lose you. You died at least once. It was scary for them. You might technically be their boss," he said it like it was a question, to which I nodded. "You're still their sister, and they love you."

I knew he was right, but it sure as hell didn't feel like it after what Santi said to me earlier.

Finishing the rest of the wine in my glass, I signaled for the waiter. "Let's not talk about my family. It will only put me in a bad mood, and that's the reason why we're here to begin with. Why don't you tell me what you're going to school for?"

"Really?" He chuckled, lacing his fingers together and placing them over his taut stomach. We should have gone to a hotel and fucked until we couldn't move anymore and then ordered room service, but I wanted a sense of normalcy. I should have known it wouldn't work. All I wanted to do was see Sebastian naked and thrusting inside of me with his mouth parted in a sexy 'O'.

I waited until my wine glass was full, and the waiter was several feet away before I spoke. "I figure small talk while eating should be safe."

In all actuality, what little I knew about Sebastian, it shocked me he was going to school. He was stealing to survive before he met up with Ale and Army.

His light brown eyes bore into mine. "And what are we going to do once we leave here?"

Tapping my fingernail on the rim of my wineglass,

I took in his broad chest and bulging biceps and licked my lips. I knew what was underneath, and I wanted it. It had been too long. "I wouldn't be opposed to finding a nice hotel to stay at for the night."

Sebastian leaned forward, putting his elbows on the table, and clasping his hands underneath his chin. "Is that so your brothers don't find out?"

While the words had never been spoken, it was understood that my brothers weren't to find out about us having sex. I was sure they had their suspicions—not that I cared.

"I don't care if they do." And I didn't. Especially not now. Nothing good came when the people you were supposed to trust the most were keeping secrets from you. "If you want, I can text them right now and tell them we'll be staying in the city overnight so you can fuck my brains out."

Sebastian's lips twitched. "That's not necessary."

"But?" There was more. I knew it.

"Then maybe Armando won't be trying to get me to fuck every chick that crosses our paths."

"You didn't think to say you're fucking someone already?" I liked that he was already so loyal to our family. It wasn't common for us to let outsiders in, but I knew I had made the right choice with Sebastian. I even kept my best friend at arm's length to a certain extent. Our lives were dangerous enough without having to worry about those we surrounded ourselves with. That's why Bree was perfect. Her father supplied the pharmaceutical portion of our business. She wasn't involved with her family business, but she knew about it and ours.

bash

WE SAT at a table that could seat ten. Arely was at the head of the table with her brother, Pablo, at the other end. I was on Arely's right with Santiago on her left. A petite Asian woman named Bree sat to his Santi's right. Ale sat beside Bree with Army to his left, and next to him was his girlfriend, the one he met the other night.

"When was the last time we all sat down for Sunday dinner together?" Ale asked his twin.

Army looked at his girl and shrugged. "It's been months."

"We should do it more often," Santiago suggested.

"Every Sunday from now on, we'll sit here, catch up, and have a brief meeting about business," Arely announced. "If you bring someone to dinner, they can hang out in the library or something during our meeting."

Her message was loud and clear. Devi, Army's newest girlfriend, wasn't going to be in the room for the meeting. I wasn't even sure if I was invited or not. I guess I'd find out.

There were head nods from everyone except the twins. Santi looked to Bree with knitted brows while Pablo stared at his sister from the other end of the table.

Two people dressed in all black started to bring in platter after platter of food. There were enchiladas, elote, chilaquiles, tamales, and a heaping bowl of guacamole with two large bowls of homemade chips.

Each platter was passed around as we piled all the amazing-smelling food onto our plates. Once I had filled my plate, I leaned over to Arely and spoke. "Is this normal?"

"For Sunday dinner, yes. Next time it will be something else, or we can vote on what cuisine we want."

We all started to dig into all the amazing food. There were multiple rounds of groans and moans.

I had just taken a long drag of my beer when Santi set down his silverware and cleared his throat. "Alright, are you ever going to tell us what's going on between the two of you?" I nearly spit out my beer when I saw his eyes were on Arely and me.

"What's there to say?" She shrugged like it was no big deal. "Sebastian and I are fucking. If you don't like it, keep your mouth shut since I've never said a single word about anyone you all were fucking."

Ale sat up taller in his seat and turned to look at his sister. "How long has this been going on?"

"Since before I met you and Army." He started to open his mouth but closed it as I kept speaking. "When I met the two of you, I had no idea you were her brothers."

Pablo leaned forward with a snarl on his upper lip. "How the hell did the two of you meet? I don't see Arely hanging around the university looking for a hookup."

Arely threw her head back and laughed. It didn't escape my notice when her hand went to where she'd been shot. "Do you think I'm so desperate that I'd be looking to hook up with college students?"

"I don't know. All you do is work, so it's possible." Santi laughed before he jumped and then yelled. "Why the fuck did you kick me? You've got those murder boots on," he pouted.

"Because you're an asshole, and if you say something like that again, I'm going to impale your shin with my heel," Arely growled. Her eyes were like lasers as she looked at everyone else at the table, willing one of them to speak up.

"You've got no complaints from me. I think Bash is cool." Army's eyes widened. "Unless you expect me to call him Papi or some shit like that. That's where I draw the line."

Now it was my turn to laugh.

One day we'd have to tell him he has to start calling me dad just to get a reaction out of him. It would be hilarious.

"I sure as fuck am not calling this pendejo anything," Pablo growled. "You shouldn't get used to him, though. He didn't pass his test," he arched a brow.

Santi stood and placed his hands on the table as he leaned toward Pablo at the other end of the table. I wasn't sure what the deal was between Pablo and the rest of them, but there was something. He was always angry. "The society isn't claiming they tried to kill Arely. If Bash suddenly ends up dead, it will only prove that they tried to kill one of their own. And then, we'll kill them."

Pablo chuckled as he shook his head. "You can't kill everyone in the society." His eyes flicked to mine. "If that wasn't indeed your test, expect another one soon. And this time, you better pass."

"Or what, they kill me?" I wasn't sure if it was all talk or not, but I wasn't going to let some fuckers kill me because I didn't pass a test.

Santiago's mouth turned down as he looked me over. "It can be deadly not to pass, but I wouldn't worry about it. Especially not now when it's been made to look like you were supposed to kill a member. Your next test will probably be easy."

"What if I don't want any part in this? Do I get a say?"

"Don't worry about it." Arely's hand gripped my knee under the table. "Like Santi said, I'm sure they'll go easy on you next time. Now that everyone's done eating, Bree, could you show Devi to the library or out back while we have our meeting?" Bree nodded and stood. "We shouldn't be long, and then you're all free to stay or go do whatever you want." Arely pushed back her chair and stood. "Let's go to my office." Her eyes followed her friend and Army's girlfriend out of the room. "Just in case."

I trailed behind and watched as Arely led the way to her office, which was right beside her bedroom. She really did work too much. Pablo and Santi quietly argued the entire way while Ale and Army were joking with one another. At first, I wasn't sure if I was supposed to be a part of this meeting, so I was shocked when I saw Arely standing inside the door to her office waiting for me. Did she trust me enough to let me in on whatever was going to be said? Once I was through the door, she closed it and went to sit behind her desk. Everyone was quiet as we all looked at one another, waiting for someone to speak or for something to happen.

"I need updates. This is how it's going to be from now on. Every Sunday, you're going to inform me of what's going on in your area. I don't want to be bothered by it during the week unless there's an emergency."

Everyone nodded their heads in agreement.

"As you know, things have slowed down at the skate park and not because Bash isn't there as much. The crowd has dried up, and now we're hitting up as many parties as we can to sell," Ale informed the room.

"Now that Bash is your fuck buddy and your bodyguard, will he be selling anymore?" Army threw out into the room.

"That's up to Sebastian what he wants to do and how busy Santi is. While we're on the topic of people we're fucking, let's talk about Devi." Arely leaned forward with her hands clasped out in front of her. Her dark brown eyes drilled into her brother's.

"What about her?" Armando started to pace back

and forth in front of her desk. "Are you going to tell me she's not good enough for me?"

"I think she's the wrong girl for you, but we're going to use her to our advantage," Arely smirked. The smile was evil, and it immediately caught my attention. Something wasn't right.

Her words caught Armando off guard, causing him to stop abruptly and turn to his sister. "What the hell are you talking about?"

"Your little girlfriend isn't who she says she is. She's playing you, Army."

"You're lying," he yelled, looking to everyone in the room for support.

"Unfortunately, I'm not. I had Santi do a background check, and it wasn't until yesterday that he finally struck gold." She looked at Santi and nodded.

"She was too clean, man. Not that a college student should have a rap sheet a mile long or anything, but there was hardly anything on her anywhere, even her social media. So, I did some more digging because it was too nicely wrapped up in a pretty little package for me, and that's when I finally struck gold. She's not a college student at all. She's been playing you this entire time. Didn't you think it was odd she was so understanding of everything?"

"I don't share jack shit with her, so there's nothing

to be understanding about. I don't even sell when she's around." Army hung his head and then shook it. "If she's not in college, then what is she?"

"D… E… A…" Arely said, slowly letting it sink in.

They couldn't be serious. How did she let Devi, or whatever her name was, into her house, knowing who she was?

"You're wrong," Army spat, but I could see in his eyes that there was a spark of knowledge there.

Santi picked up a folder off the desk and threw it to Army. "See for yourself."

Army caught it and sank into a chair as he looked over the pages. He sunk lower and lower with each page turned until his eyes came up to meet Arely's. "I had no idea."

"I know you didn't. I want you to work her. Get her to trust you, but don't share anything with her that will come back to hurt us. When she leaves you, I want her followed to see where she goes and who she's informing." Army nodded woodenly. "Bug her. Do whatever you have to do, so we know what they know. We aren't flying under the radar anymore."

"Fuck," Ale and Army growled at the same time.

Knowing she did a background check on Devi made me wonder if she had one done on me as well. It didn't matter since I didn't have anything to hide. She knew I grew up with no money and did whatever I had to do to survive. Arely knew that about me from day one.

"If no one has anything else to share, let's go and enjoy the rest of the night." Arely stood behind her desk, looking commanding as she looked over everyone in the room.

Arely being in charge of both a drug cartel and her family was hot as hell. All I wanted to do was pull her into the next room and fuck her senseless.

I waited until the room cleared to prowl toward her. Picking Arely up, she instantly wrapped her legs around my waist as I bent and took her mouth in a searing kiss.

She pulled away, her breath heavy with want. "Do business meetings turn you on?"

"You turn me on. Being all commanding and in charge has my dick so hard for you right now. I need to fuck you," I growled. Opening the door that led to her bedroom, I pressed her up against the door. Gripping her shirt on each side, I pulled, ripping it down the center. I didn't have time to remove clothes. I wanted my face buried in her succulent tits.

My hands moved under her skirt, and when I found her pussy covered, I ripped the fabric and plunged two fingers deep inside of her. "From now on, I don't want you wearing underwear. I want to be able to slip inside of you whenever I want."

Pulling my fingers out, she whimpered but quickly recovered. Her hands went straight to the button on my jeans. She had my dick out and was running her slick pussy over it in no time. Wrapping her arms around my neck, Arely lowered herself until my dick was fully sheathed by her tight, hot pussy. I groaned, pulling back and then slammed back into her already quaking core. Arely rode my dick like her life depended on it. Her mouth was frantic on mine. Our teeth clashed together, and I tasted blood. It only seemed to spur Arely on. Our tongues dueled, sliding against the other. Probing, tasting, and fucking each other's mouths. Even as she came apart, she kept up her pace. Riding me hard and grinding down as her pussy walls strangled my dick. I wouldn't last much longer. Coating my thumb with her juices, I slipped it into her ass, wanting her to come once more. We came at the same time, moaning into each other's mouths. I pressed her further into the door, pinning her there as I worked the last of our orgasms out of us.

I loved that she wasn't soft when I fucked her. There was nothing soft about Arely. She was pure fire, and I couldn't get enough of her, even knowing one day I'd be burned.

arely

THREE ORGASMS LATER, I breathed heavily into Sebastian's neck. His arms were still clasped around me as our heart rates slowly started to return to back to normal when my bedroom door flew open.

"Oh shit," Santi shielded his eyes and turned around to face the door. "If you two could stop fucking for a minute, we have an emergency."

Sebastian's arms slipped down my back and pulled my silk sheets up until I was covered. Only then did he slip out from under me to glare at my brother for his intrusion. "Have you ever heard of knocking?"

"We have more important things to discuss than manners in my own home," Santi growled as he paced around my room.

Turning, I held the sheet to my chest. "This is *my*

home—something you would all do well to remember. If you give me a few minutes to get dressed, I'll meet you in my office. Is this something everyone should be in attendance for?"

"Everyone is assembled in your office waiting for you. I texted you over an hour ago." His jaw ticked as he opened the door that led to my office. "Multiple times. You were too busy to respond, I guess."

"Very busy indeed." I could hear the smirk in Sebastian's tone. I wasn't sure what their problem was, but they needed to get over it. Neither of them was going anywhere anytime soon, and if they made me choose, they wouldn't like the consequences.

"Just hurry up. Don't make a detour on your way to your office," Santi grumbled before he slipped out of the room.

Climbing out of bed, I headed straight for the shower. I wasn't going to sit across from my brothers with Sebastian's cum dripping out of me. I was a little classier than that—not much, but some. I stepped under the cold water and didn't wait for it to warm up. Whatever was going on had to be important; otherwise, Santi would never have barged into my room.

Sebastian stepped inside, only for me to push him out. "What the hell, Arely? Are you really not going to let me rinse off?"

I ran my soapy hands over my body and removed the overhead sprayer. "You are not coming in here with me. If you do, it will probably take us another hour to see what they want, and I really don't feel like having another one of my brothers seeing me naked." Cleaning between my legs, I nearly came when the warm water came into contact with my clit. It was so damn sensitive, and it would only take a moment for me to come. Too bad I didn't have time for that.

Sebastian continued to stand there with his arms crossed over his chest. The move made his biceps and pecs flex in the most delicious way. He watched as my body shuddered before I put the sprayer back. "Have you ever gotten yourself off with your shower attachment?"

Turning off the water, I wrapped a warm, white towel around me before I stepped out and headed to my closet. "Many times. Do you have a problem with that?"

"No, more power to you. I was just thinking about how hot you would be getting yourself off. Maybe later we can take a shower together since I'm still dirty, and you can show me." The deep, husky tone of his voice had me wanting to drop my towel and get back under the shower spray. When Sebastian was around, I could never get enough. It was safe to say I was addicted to his dick and all the orgasms he gave me daily. It didn't help that he had the body of a bronzed god and knew how to use it. Sebastian King was my kryptonite.

Pulling out the first set of underwear I came across, I tried my hardest not to look at his naked form. "Right now, we need to focus on whatever the emergency is. In fact, you need to get dressed now unless you plan to walk in naked."

"Fine," he grumbled as he left the closet. Sebastian was digging into the bag he brought when he showed up last night. I wasn't sure what he was looking for because there wasn't room in it to have more than a few items, and they were all scattered on my bed. At least he had pulled on a pair of jeans. He'd left the top button unbuttoned, and for some unknown reason, it was damn hot. I wanted to pull his zipper down with my teeth and take his thick cock into my mouth.

"You shouldn't look at me like that," he said, bringing me out of my musing. "It's already hard enough to contain myself around you with you eye fucking me across the room."

"Let's go." I walked to the door that connected my office to my bedroom and opened it. Sebastian was right behind me, pulling a t-shirt over his head.

All eyes were on us as we stepped into my office,

except for Santi. Maybe he'd think twice about not knocking after today.

"It's about fucking time," Army huffed. "I was getting ready to meet up with Devi when this pendejo messaged us all for an emergency." Army signaled to Santi.

"How's it going with her?" I asked as I sat behind my desk. "Have you learned anything yet?"

"So far, she hasn't met up with anyone or planted any bugs. I'm keeping a close eye on her, though."

"Good, keep it up. We can't let the DEA learn anything about us." I looked at Santi with raised brows. "What's the emergency?"

"We've had a few ODs in the last couple of weeks, and I did some digging. I had a batch of our last shipment tested, and there's fentanyl in our coke. Anyone want to tell me how that happened? It's bad enough the DEA is on us, but if more people OD on our shit, they are going to be crawling up our asses. We can't have that."

I shifted to look at Pablo. "Is there any way we can trace who it came from?"

"Maybe we need to make a trip down to Colombia and remind them who they're fucking with?" Santi suggested.

Pablo steepled his fingers in front of his face and

nodded. A dark look crossed his face. "We can make a vacation out of it. It's been too long since we've been there. I think it's time we remind them who they're working for and what will happen if they fuck us over."

It would be nice, but I wasn't sure it was the right move. "Are we sure it's on their end and not here?" It didn't make sense the cooks in Colombia could get their hands on fentanyl.

"The twins can stay here and work with their guys. Your boyfriend too, if it will make you feel better," Pablo smirked, knowing I'd hate the idea of leaving them behind.

"Make the arrangements for us all to go as soon as possible. I don't want any more deaths associated with our drugs. While they may be risking their lives doing coke, they are not prepared for fentanyl."

"I'll get on it right away." Pablo looked to Santi. "How many guards are you planning on bringing with us?"

Santi chewed on the inside of his cheek for a moment before his eyes lit up. "One for each of us. I think if we have more, it will draw too much attention with the transport."

I agreed. We needed to stay as compact as possible on the streets we'd be traveling. Having two guys for each of us would cause a scene.

I looked around the room. "Is there anything else?"

"Yeah, how long until he's living here?" Ale asked with a chuckle.

"What?" I laughed, looking toward Sebastian.

"Yeah, he's always here," Army added.

"He's protecting me when Santi's not."

"And fucking your brains out every other second," Army chuckled and flipped Sebastian off. "I don't mind if he's living here. You asked if there was anything else, and we wanted to know."

"It's good to know some of you approve, but that's between Sebastian and me. If that's all, I have some work to do if we're going to be headed to Colombia soon."

One by one, they each came to kiss me on the cheek before they left the room. Sebastian was the last, and he lingered by the door. "You don't have to come if you don't want to. I understand if you don't want to miss your classes."

"You think I give a shit about class?" He shook his head as he came toward me. "I want to be there to protect you. Colombia is not a safe country to be in."

I sat back in my chair. "Is that all it is? You want to protect me?"

He sat on the edge of my desk and took one of my hands in his. "I like you, Arely. You should know that by now. If something were to happen to you and I wasn't there, I'm not sure how I'd live with myself."

"You shouldn't put that stress on yourself. I knowingly put myself in this danger from the start." Griping his hand, I looked into his troubled eyes. "You had no idea what you were getting involved in when you started this. I won't hold you to my protection."

"Damn it, Arely, I can't help it. I'm as drawn to protecting you as I am fucking you. Don't try to stop me."

I nodded, understanding.

There was something about Sebastian that drew me to him. It didn't matter if I wanted it or not. I knew his life would be better off without me in it, and yet I couldn't push him away. Instead, I brought him closer with each passing day.

"Come with me." I stood and walked into my bedroom and straight to my closet. I opened a drawer in my dresser that sat in the middle and left it open for him to look inside.

I watched as he fingered the contents inside before he looked at me over the dresser. "Why is there a gun in here?"

"It's for you. If you are to help guard me, you need a gun on you at all times, and you can fill up that drawer with your belongings. If you're going to be here as often as you have been, then you shouldn't have to live out of that tiny bag."

Pulling his hand out of the drawer like it bit him, Sebastian walked around the dresser like a lion on the hunt, and I was his prey. He could be the king of my jungle any time. "Are you asking me to move in with you?"

"No," I stepped closer to him. I would never step back when he was near. "This is me saying you can leave some things here to make your life easier. That is all."

Reaching up, one fingertip traced my jaw. His thumb pressed into my bottom lip as his eyes searched mine. "It feels like more than that."

I bit the tip of his thumb and then ran my tongue over it. "It's for the selfish reason of being able to keep you in my bed longer." Shifting closer, I unzipped his jeans and slipped my hand inside to find his cock already stiffening. I ran my palm up and down his growing length. "What do you say we take that shower now?"

His normally light eyes darkened as he pushed his jeans down his legs and stepped out of them. His long, thick cock slapped against his abs and bobbed as he moved. He pulled his t-shirt over his head and let it drop to the floor. I followed suit, removing my clothes as I walked through my bedroom and into the bathroom. I couldn't take my eyes off Sebastian as his muscles flexed while turning on the shower. He stood underneath the cold spray, and I watched entranced as trails of water sluiced down his perfect body. I wanted to lick each and every drop.

Stepping forward, he held his hand out to me. "Am I going to have to come out there and get you?"

"As much as I'd love for you to chase me, I'd much rather get wet and dirty with you now." Unclasping my bra, I slid the straps down my arms and let the garment fall to the floor at my feet. Taking Sebastian's hand, I let him pull me under the now warm spray and melded my body to his. His lips brushed against my shoulder and moved up the side of my neck to my waiting mouth. The second our mouths connected, it was like a shot of lightning stuck us both. My hands skated down his torso to his treasure trail that led to the promised land. His cock rested against my stomach as his hands cupped my ass and brought us flesh to flesh.

His hands kneaded the globes of my ass as I kissed every inch of him I could. "Fuck, you've got the best damn ass I've ever seen. Not today, but soon, I'm going to claim that sweet ass of yours."

Wrapping my leg around his hip, I guided his cock between my legs and started to rock. "Yes," I moaned.

"I love how hungry your pussy is for my dick. Turn around," Sebastian ordered at the same time he gripped my shoulders and brought my back to his front. One of his large hands cupped and massaged my breasts, while the other slowly trailed down from my sternum all the way to where I wanted him most. Two fingers dipped inside of me, pumping twice before pulling out.

"More," I moaned.

Raking his stubble up my neck, he stopped at the shell of my ear. His voice was gravelly as he spoke. "So much more. Grab the sprayer and show me what you do to yourself with it."

I did as he wanted and took the sprayer off the wall and turned the dial until the water was coming out like a jet. The feel of his hard body against my back already had me on edge. I was so worked up it wouldn't take much for the water to set me off.

Widening my stance, I lowered the showerhead until the warm water blasted between my legs and came into contact with my clit. My body jolted at the pleasure. My other hand curved around Sebastian's hip and gripped his ass.

"I won't last long," I shuddered as I moved the sprayer back and forth.

He pushed me forward until my front was pressed

up against the cool tiles. The dueling sensations of the tiles and the warmth of the water and Sebastian at my back had my body overloaded. I needed more.

As if he could read my mind, I felt his cock nudge at my entrance only seconds before he thrust his hips and was fully inside. I let out a long moan. My pussy quivered and stretched at the fullness he always provided. Using the sprayer, I hit us where we were connected, and it set Sebastian off.

A low growl unfurled from deep in his chest as he pulled back and slammed into me time after time. My free hand moved to claw at the walls trying to find purchase. He felt too good inside of me. Each thrust brought me closer and closer to the promised land.

His rough hand gripped my hip and angled me in a way that only made me feel him deeper. Pulling the water from where we were joined, I hit my clit and nearly came on the spot.

"Whatever you're doing, keep doing it," he panted in my ear. "The way your pussy just clenched around my cock was nothing short of spectacular. I want to feel you grip me like a vice and never let go until you've milked me of every last drop of cum."

Turning my head and angling it up, I pressed my lips to his, opening up when his tongue probed inside. I gripped his neck with my free hand and let him fuck my mouth the same way he was fucking my pussy.

When we were like this, there was no outside world. There was only him and me. Our bodies moved together in tandem like they were made for each other, making me wish for our joining to never end.

Tingles slowly spread from the nape of my neck down to my toes while at the same time lighting a fire inside of me. I pressed the water closer to my nub, knowing it would set me off while Sebastian continued to crash into me from behind. And just like that, the world stopped. I arched into him, and he ate the scream that came out of my mouth. My entire body quaked as I rode higher and higher, clenching around his cock, never wanting to let it go. I could happily die with Sebastian inside of me, claiming me the way that he was. It was freeing and addictive.

Pulling me back from the wall, he took the sprayer and brought it straight to my highly sensitized clit, and held it there. His other arm bound around me like he was holding me together while he continued to piston inside of me. It was all too much. When I didn't think it could get much better, my pleasure intensified. Breaking apart, I let out a soundless cry, and my body exploded like a supernova. My eyes were open but unseeing as white, hot pleasure coursed through my body.

I felt it when the water dropped away from my center. My body instantly sagged against his. If it wasn't for his strong grip on me, I had no doubt I would have been a puddle on my shower floor. My head lolled back in time to see Sebastian's mouth part in the sexiest 'O' face I'd ever seen. The feel of his hot cum releasing inside of me had my walls constricting around him once again. My pussy was greedy for every last drop. I wanted it all.

We stood there for a long moment. I wasn't sure how long. My body shook with aftershocks while Sebastian held me tight to his body, and he breathed heavily into the top of my head. I wondered if he was as spent as I was.

Eventually, he picked me up in his arms. I nuzzled into his neck, wrapping my arms around him. I was so close to falling asleep that I barely felt it as he wrapped me in a towel. I only knew we were walking when I felt the cool air hit my overheated skin. A second later, I was being wrapped in blankets with Sebastian at my back.

I turned, resting my cheek on his chest and molding my front to his. I wanted every inch of us that we could to be touching. With his arms around me, he pulled me closer. My leg went between his as I slowly started to fade away.

This was perfect, but I knew it wouldn't stay that way. I knew in that moment I would fight heaven and hell to keep what we had. It may have just been the beginning, but it was everything, and I wouldn't let him go.

bash

WHILE I KNEW ARELY and her family had money, I had no idea they had private plane kind of money. The inside was all white and gold, making you feel like you were ensconced in luxury. The plush leather seats were soft and molded perfectly to your body. If I could live on this plane, I would.

I sat by the window, looking out at the world below me. I'd never flown before, nor had I left the country, and today I was doing both in style.

Arely, Santiago, and Pablo were in the back having a meeting while Ale and Army sat on a couch playing a video game and fighting about who was cheating. The rest of the seats were filled by the guards that were brought for our protection.

When I woke up this morning, a passport sat on the

bedside table with a note to pack and be ready in an hour. I wasn't sure how they got me a passport so fast. It was only five days since they decided to make the trip, but I wasn't going to question it. Two hours later, we were boarding their plane.

"Enjoying the view?" came Arely's honeyed voice as she sat down beside me.

"I've never flown before," I muttered as I continued to look out the window.

She ran one lone fingernail from my hand up my arm and circled back down. "You should have said something, and I wouldn't have left you to your own devices during takeoff. I'm guessing since no one said anything, you didn't mind the takeoff."

I caught her hand in mine as I shifted to look at her. "I was fine. The reason for never flying wasn't because I thought I would freak out. It was merely the fact that I never had any money or any place to go."

She gave me a small, almost innocent smile. Except there was nothing innocent about Arely. She was a hardcore badass. She probably came out of the womb that way. "I know it might seem like I've always lived like this, but I haven't—only the twins. When I was young, we were poor. My two brothers and I lived in a one-bedroom apartment with our parents. I don't remember much since I was so young, but I remember my father working night and day to provide for us. He started at the bottom and worked his way up to being the boss." She blinked, coming back into focus, and looked at me. "I'm not naïve. I'm sure he killed people to get where he was. That's the price you pay for living in this world."

Arely was right. I would never have guessed at any point in her life she'd been poor. Maybe she could appreciate where I came from.

"Be prepared for a culture shock and be on your toes. Some of the places we're going are violent. That's the only way of life they know."

Why was she telling me this?

"You haven't had any training, but I want you to remain vigilant. Keep your eyes peeled for anything. If you think something is wrong or going down, tell someone. Anyone in our group."

"I won't let you down," I vowed.

She leaned forward, her eyes locked with mine. "I know you won't." Sitting back in her seat, Arely closed her eyes and relaxed.

"How did your meeting go?"

She kept her eyes closed as she spoke in a low, unaffected tone. "One of the worst parts about working with family is the fighting. We fight about *everything.*

Each of us thinks we're right and doesn't want to back down."

"So, it went how you expected it to go." I looked back out the window and to the water below.

"It did." This time, she sounded exhausted.

"Why don't you get some sleep before we land," I suggested.

"Good idea."

I thought she was going to lean her chair back like I'd seen some of the guards do, but instead, Arely curled up on her side and rested her head against my arm. It felt like only a matter of seconds before she relaxed against me and her breaths slowed. One of the stewardesses came by with a blanket and placed it over Arely. She snuggled in closer and let out a contented sigh.

I was lost in the heat emanating off her body and her soft breaths when Ale spoke, breaking me out of my trancelike state. My brows furrowed as I tried to make out what he'd said. "She looks good on you. I've never seen her happier or more relaxed than when she's with you."

"But if you hurt her, we'll kill you, and you know that isn't an idle threat. We. Will. Kill. You," Army said like he was talking about the weather, not my demise.

If Arely hadn't been using me for a pillow, I

would've gotten up and in their faces. Almost as if she could feel me tensing, her arm wrapped around my middle.

"I don't plan on hurting her," I clipped out. I had no idea where this was going with Arely or my place in their world, but I knew it wasn't going to be as easy as it had been. "But let's get one thing straight. You won't be taking me down if something does happen."

"Oh, listen to the big words from the *big* man. He thinks just because he's sleeping with the boss, he's calling the shots." Army laughed bitterly.

"Shut up, all of you," Arely spoke in a deadly calm voice I hadn't heard from her before. It seemed her brothers had, though. They shut their mouths and looked the other way. The entire time, she kept her eyes closed and looked as if she was sleeping against my arm.

Leaning close, I spoke quietly for only her to hear. "Arely, I—"

This time, one eye peeked open, and the fire burning in that one eye had me hard in a nanosecond. "Don't."

I only wanted to tell her I wasn't going to take their shit because they were her brothers. I wouldn't take it from anyone. Not even her, but now I had other ideas.

Taking the hand from around my waist, I ran it

down my abs and to the growing bulge in my pants. "Does this plane have a bedroom in the back?"

"It does, but we are not going to use it," she said simply.

Even at her denial, my dick didn't listen. He grew harder as I cupped her hand over the straining fabric.

One corner of my mouth tipped up before she spoke. "If you want, you can head back and jack yourself off in the bathroom."

"No help from you? That doesn't sound nearly as fun." I wasn't ruled by my dick, but I was twenty years old. Even with all the sex we'd been having, I was always down for more.

"Fun times are over for now. You'll have to wait until—"

"I have no problem waiting for you." I removed her hand, placed it on my stomach, and covered it with my own.

"Good. Why don't you get some rest? You're going to need it. We're going to be very busy the next few days, and I need you in tip-top shape."

Arely was right. I couldn't protect her if I was dragging. Wrapping my arm around her, I leaned my seat back. With the seat molded to my body and Arely's body heat at my side, it didn't take long for me to start to doze off.

It felt like a matter of minutes when my eyes popped open, and our plane was descending. I wasn't going to lie. I was excited to visit another country, even if it was one that was as dangerous as Colombia. I wasn't under the impression we wouldn't run into trouble. I knew it would happen. I just didn't know how or when.

Looking to my right, Arely was sitting upright and talking to Santi. The second his eyes landed on mine, he clapped her on the shoulder and walked to the back of the plane.

"He doesn't like me," I stated. Hell, it felt like the twins were starting to not like me. Maybe it was because I wasn't under their control any longer.

Pulling her hair to the side, she ran her fingers through her long tresses. "He doesn't like many people outside of our family. Plus, he's afraid we're getting too close, and I'm going to get hurt."

"I don't plan to hurt you."

"I know that. If I thought that was your plan, you wouldn't be here or in my bed. We're getting close, and feelings are bound to develop." Her brown eyes bore into mine as if willing me to spill my deepest, darkest secrets.

Did her words mean she had feelings for me?

Before I could ask, we touched down with a slight

jerk of the plane. The second we stopped, everyone was up and out of their seats. The guards headed off the plane, where they immediately went to three black Suburbans sitting on the tarmac. They scanned every inch of each vehicle before Javier stepped back onto the plane.

"All clear. We'll get the luggage, and then we'll head to the hotel. It will be the same protocol as when we were in New York. You will all wait in your vehicle until we check each room." He nodded once and then slipped back off the plane.

"So that's where you went," Ale laughed.

"If you wanted to know so badly, you could have asked me. I have nothing to hide."

Army's face scrunched up. "None of us have anything to hide from each other. That's what makes our family work."

"Someone is hiding something," Arely whispered to herself. I wasn't sure if I was meant to hear what she said or not. Was she telling me to be on the lookout even with her own family because someone couldn't be trusted? I wanted to ask her about it, but it would have to wait until we were alone. If she suspected something, why would she bring whoever it was along? Was it so they wouldn't know Arely was questioning a member of her family?

Taking up my place behind Arely, I watched each member on the plane. If Arely didn't trust them, neither would I.

Now I had to be more vigilant than ever in keeping her safe with this new knowledge.

arely

AT FIRST, when Sebastian insisted on being my bodyguard, I placated him. Santi was all I needed, or so I thought, but as I watched him keep a constant vigil on the streets around us, I knew he wouldn't let anything happen to me.

I could tell he was shocked by the conditions of the areas we traveled through. While many parts of Colombia were beautiful, there were double as many that were dirty, poor, and violent.

That was my world.

We left our gorgeous hotel with the best views to traverse through the poorest parts of Medellín, then out into the country to visit one of our labs. They had no idea we were coming. Well, that wasn't true, I was sure word was out that we were in the country, causing great panic.

Leaning over, Sebastian spoke so quietly, I could barely hear him over everyone else talking. "Do you really think they'll admit to putting fentanyl in the product?"

My body gravitated toward the heat he was emanating. I simply couldn't help myself. Putting my hand on his golden, bronzed arm, I locked eyes with him. "Not if they want to live, but they need to know we're onto them."

He leaned closer this time. So close, I could feel his breath across my neck with each word he spoke. I closed my eyes, remembering the same feeling when I woke up this morning with Sebastian curled around me —his body was always protecting mine, even in our sleep. "And what if it wasn't them?"

If it wasn't, I would find out who it was and end them. It didn't matter who it was.

"Word will get out, and whoever it is *will* be scared. I will not let anyone destroy me and my family."

Sebastian nodded and then looked over my shoulder. I knew who was watching us. Santi was always watching. My best friend was slipping away.

"What's his problem?"

Running the tips of my nails along his arm, I shifted closer to him in the backseat of the SUV. "They're not used to seeing me with anyone. It's going to take them a while to get used to the idea."

His eyes grew dark, liking the idea.

"I keep my sex life out of my home for the most part. I don't let just anyone in."

And yet I'd let Sebastian in without a second thought.

A shot rang out. It was close. All eyes turned to the windows as we canvased the area looking for where it might have come from.

"Shit," Santi yelled from the front passenger seat. "Behind."

An explosion sent a shock wave through our vehicle. My ears rang as I turned to see what Santi had seen. Behind us, the second Suburban with our extra guards sat on fire in the middle of the street.

"Ve," Santi shouted.

"Dónde?" Our driver shouted back with a quiver in his voice.

"I don't know, just lose them and take us somewhere safe," Santi hissed.

"Somewhere they won't be expecting us," Sebastian shot out.

"What about other car?" The driver asked as he took a sharp left.

"They'll find their own way." Santi turned in his seat, looking out the back. "Más rápido."

Gunshots rang out into the sticky air. I could hear them hitting our SUV and silently prayed we would make it out of here.

Sebastian pushed me down and practically laid on top of me as the tires of our SUV screeched. I felt the driver accelerate as he tried to break away.

I could feel my phone buzzing in my pocket, but there was no way for me to answer it. I was frozen in fear as shot after shot rang out and pelted our SUV.

"Be prepared to shoot," Santi yelled. I could hear the panic in his voice. Something I hadn't heard in… forever. Santi was always calm, cool, and collected. We both were, but in that moment, I was scared. I didn't want to die.

The next few minutes were a series of turns that threw Sebastian and me from one side of the SUV to the other. I'd lost track of how many times we turned.

"I think we lost them." Santi's voice sounded both far away and close.

I tried to sit up, wanting to see for myself that we were safe, but Sebastian wouldn't let me up. He grunted when I elbowed him in the stomach but held fast.

"Stay down, Arely," he gritted out.

"It's over." I tried to push up using all my strength, but I was no match for Sebastian or his weight.

"Let's play this safe. I'll get off you, but you need to stay down just in case."

The second his weight started to shift, I pushed up and twisted to look out the back. We were in the middle of nowhere on some one-lane road speeding past green fields. My body instantly started to shake, the shock starting to wear off.

Sebastian grabbed me by the side of the neck and pushed me down until my head was resting in his lap. Closing my eyes, I let him hold me down this time and wrapped my hand around his thigh. Being connected to him helped ease the growing dread that started to slither in my stomach.

If we didn't play this right, I was going to die, and quite possibly my brothers as well.

"Hey, asshole, this isn't the time for my sister to be giving you a blow job," Santi growled.

My eyes sprung open, and my hand shot out, punching Santi in the arm. "Shut the fuck up, and call the others to see if they're okay."

My body started to shake for a whole different reason.

What if they didn't make it?

Rotating toward Sebastian, I buried my face into his stomach. As much as I tried to hold back the wetness that started to build, I couldn't. Not with the possibility that Pablo, Ale, and Army might be dead.

Sebastian's hand cupped the back of my head and started to run his fingers through my hair slowly. He didn't tell me it was going to be okay, and I was thankful he didn't make any promises he couldn't keep.

"Arely," Santi said my name so quietly I was terrified to hear his next words. They could either break me or set me free of the terror building inside of me. "They're all fine. We're going to figure out a place to meet up where no one will be able to find us."

I nodded, not wanting to let him see me weak. He patted my hip, and then I heard him turn around. Santi and the driver spoke back and forth about options on where we could go for the night. The entire time, Sebastian ran his fingers through my hair. I wasn't sure how he knew what I needed, but the way his fingers played with my hair put me in a trancelike state. All I could do was feel his touch, making it seem as if there was no outside world beyond our little bubble.

Halfway between sleep and awake, I felt the car jerk

to a stop. Instantly, I was on alert. My body tensed, ready for anything that might come our way. Sitting up, I looked around, taking in my new surroundings. The sun was further west than I expected. How long had we been driving?

"We should get inside. The rest will be here in about twenty minutes. Keep your heads down and try to look inconspicuous."

I was pretty sure that was going to be next to impossible with the three of us and our two guards. Santi always stood out in a crowd; there were no two ways about it. At least I had dressed down, thinking we were going to be traipsing through the jungle.

The second I stepped out of the SUV, I wrapped myself around Sebastian like he was a lifeline. Even though Santi had said Pablo and the twins were safe, I wouldn't fully believe it until I saw them with my own two eyes.

The moment the door opened, music spilled out, causing me to look up to see where the hell we were. There wasn't a name on the establishment, making me hesitant. Would we really be safe here?

The room was filled with tables and booths, sultry music filling the air. Barely clothed women writhed on the laps of men while they smoked and drank.

The rest of our party walked through like we

weren't in some strip joint. I continued to follow Santi and the driver as they navigated through the maze of tables. I could feel the heat of the guards directly behind me. I was sure they wondered why they took this job now that half the team was dead.

I spotted a hallway that was lined with doors. I tried to keep my head down and not make any eye contact. I wanted to be forgettable. No one could find out that we were here. Luckily, it seemed as if the patrons had more important things to watch than our brigade of misfits.

I could feel Sebastian's body start to vibrate with tension the closer we got to the hallway. Halfway down the hallway, the driver opened a door and waited for us to pile in. It was only then that I started to wonder where we'd found this driver. Was he on our side? He could have easily led us into an ambush.

Taking in the room, I realized it was a bedroom. Was this where our driver lived?

Letting go of Sebastian, I stepped to the driver. We were the same height, but he had at least seventy-five pounds on me. "What is this place?"

He smiled kindly, like we hadn't just been in a shootout not that long ago. "No need to be worried. You're safe here. No one is going to be looking for you in Sonsón, let alone a whorehouse."

A whorehouse. That made sense.

"You stay here, and I'll wait out front for the rest. Once they arrive, I'll bring them back, and we can figure out where we're going from here."

Santi nodded to one of the guards, and he followed our driver out. If we lived through this, I was going to have to find out his name and make sure he got paid handsomely for all he'd done for us.

Sebastian moved to lean against the wall with his eyes trained on the door. "Shouldn't we keep the guards with us, just in case?"

Santi's eyes slanted Sebastian's way, and he let out a huff of air. "I don't want him out there by himself on the off chance he's not trustworthy. He could be calling in the calvary, and we wouldn't know it until it's too late."

Sebastian nodded with his eyes still zeroed in on the door. "Smart thinking."

"Yes, thank you." Santi rolled his eyes. "I've been doing this for longer than two weeks. I didn't get the job because I'm fucking the boss."

Sebastian took his eyes off the door for one brief second and glanced over to where Santi was sitting on the bed. "No, you got the job because you're her fucking brother."

"Enough," I hissed out. "There's a time and a place for this shit, and it certainly isn't now. We need to figure out if this was done by rivals, whoever tainted our shipment, or the society."

Leaning forward, Santi placed his elbows on his knees and rested his chin on his clasped hands. "Do you really think the society would do it here of all places?"

"Why not?" I held my arms out at my sides. "No one would suspect them."

"No one suspects them now. They weren't who tried to kill you."

"Someone sent the test to him," I nodded toward Sebastian. "It looked exactly like all our tests. If it wasn't the Scorpio Society as a whole, it was a member. How else would they have got Sebastian's test to him and made it look authentic?"

"I'm not saying I don't believe it wasn't someone in the society, but I think it was one person. Who have you pissed off?"

I let out a bark of laughter. "Who haven't I pissed off?"

"True," he smirked for a second, and then his face fell flat. "I think today is someone different. Who? I have no clue, but I don't think we should cut our trip short."

"And back down?" I shook my head. I could feel my blood start to boil at the thought of anyone thinking we were weak. "No way in hell. That's not going to look good. We need to show we are a force not to be messed with."

"Then we need to hire more guards. An army to surround us, and until then, we need to lie low."

We were stupid to bring so few guards. We should have brought them all, but the logistics of getting them here seemed more difficult than it was worth. Now we were regretting that decision.

Easy wasn't the best way.

The door swung open to reveal Ale and Army, both trying to barrel through the door at the same time. The second they saw me, they came running through the small room and hugged me on each side.

"Thank God you're okay. When we saw that explosion..." Ale shuddered.

"We thought they got you, and then you were gone." Army held me tighter.

"Your driver was smart. No one will look for us here." Pablo eyed the room with disdain.

Yes, I didn't prefer to hide out in a room where there was no telling how many people had sex on a given day, but beggars couldn't be choosers. I was just happy we'd all made it out alive.

Pablo sat down next to Santi on the bed and hung his head. "What are we doing now?"

"I'm calling in the calvary—all the guys we have in New York and more from here. From now on, we're going to have an army behind us. I should have anticipated this. They probably saw we only had a few guards with us and decided now would be the perfect time to take us out."

Pablo's heavy brows furrowed. "Who?"

"I don't know." Santi shook his head. "It could be any number of people, but we should have come here strong. I can tell you now, we are going to leave here as a force no one wants to mess with. And once I figure out who the attempt was made by, they're going to wish they'd never even thought of trying to hurt us. I'm not just going to end their life. I'm going to first ruin their family and friends' lives, and then I'm going to torture them slowly. And then torture them some more."

Pablo clapped him on the shoulder. "First, you've got to figure out who did it. Now, what are we going to do in the meantime?"

"I have spoken to the owner of the establishment, and you are welcome to stay here for as long as you need. The men are welcome to sample the ladies too while you wait."

"Free whores?" Ale laughed. "What fun. Are we all to stay in this room or—"

"Unfortunately, this is the only open room unless you're with a girl," our driver said.

Ale looked at me and frowned. "I guess you're stuck with me then, hermana."

"I'm always happy to have you, Ale. You know that."

Pablo jumped up and clapped his hands. "I don't know about the rest of you, but I'm all for some free pussy." He looked to Army and Santi. "Are you going to join me?"

Santi was already shaking his head. "You go ahead and have your fun. I've got to get more men."

Army followed Pablo to the door. "Why not? My fake girlfriend isn't here to please me."

Pablo looked back to where Sebastian was standing. He'd barely taken his eyes off the door. I wasn't sure if he was hearing what they were saying or not. "What do you say, Bash? Are you coming?"

Sebastian's only answer was to narrow his eyes and cross his arms over his chest.

Pablo laughed, shaking his head as he ushered Army out the door.

"Try not to catch any diseases while you're here," I called out as they left the room.

The room was silent for several long minutes. We were frozen until Santi pulled out his phone and started to type.

Ale looked down at the bed with his entire face scrunched up before he perched himself on the edge of the mattress. "I seriously can't believe they are out there getting their dicks wet right now."

Santi looked up from his phone with one brow raised. "Are you seriously telling us that if there were any guys out there that you wouldn't be doing the same thing?"

"You act like I'll stick my dick into any asshole that will open for me," Ale scoffed and moved further away from Santi. "That's not how it works. I won't fuck any willing man."

Sebastian pushed off the wall, and with two strides, he was standing in front of me. Taking my hand in his, he pulled me over to the one chair in the room. It was a sickly yellow color that had seen better days with hardly any cushion left in the seat. He sat down with his legs spread wide and pulled me down onto his lap.

I went willingly. Snuggling into his side and trying to let go of all the rampant thoughts of earlier fade away. Tilting my head up, I found his light brown eyes focused solely on me. They were turbulent, but I didn't blame him. He probably wished he'd never gotten involved with my family. "What's this for?"

Dipping his head down, he spoke quietly for only me to hear. His lips brushed along the shell of my ear, making my body come alive. "Because I wanted to be able to feel you in my arms to make sure you're really here."

bash

SITTING in that tiny room for days while we were waiting for more people to arrive was torture. I was itching to find out who had tried to kill Arely once again. She'd mentioned after she was shot that it was the first attempt on her life, and now there'd been another. I was starting to wonder if maybe I was bad luck for her. If I wasn't around, would she be safer?

Santi had been on the phone non-stop to bring the rest of the guards from New York down here while simultaneously trying to find people he could trust here to keep us safe.

I knew little about how their organization worked, but I was learning. The more I knew, the easier it would be for me to protect Arely and the rest of her family. Nothing could happen to her brothers. The joy that spread across her face when she saw her brothers walk through the door told me she'd be devastated if any harm came to them.

"What's the plan once they arrive? Are we still going to the lab?" Army tapped his foot impatiently. I wasn't sure why he was so anxious. He'd been with one whore or another the entire time we'd been here. The rest of us, sans Pablo, had been stuck in this room the entire time. We didn't even leave to eat. Our food was brought to us, and we used the little bathroom that was attached for the rest of our needs.

We were all on edge and bored out of our minds. I couldn't wait to escape this place. I wanted to go back to the hotel and get some real sleep other than the little I'd gotten while sitting in the chair that was now mine and Arely's. She slept fitfully on my lap for short periods of time, but mostly she paced the room, making me, Ale, and Santi dizzy.

Santi sat his phone down, and an evil smirk crossed his face. "Oh, we're going, and we're going to make sure the word spreads that if anyone fucks with us even the most minute amount, we'll kill them all. We pay our people more than anyone else, and for that, they should be loyal."

Arely slipped off my lap and started to pace the room once again with her hands on her hips. "Hell fucking yeah, they should be. If they were working for anyone else, they'd be making at least half of what we fucking pay them. After that, we're going to check into another hotel. We'll send the guards to collect our things from the other hotel."

Reclining back on the bed, Ale put his hands behind his head. "Are you saying you don't want to spend any more time in this lovely abode?

Coming back to me, Arely sat down on my leg and faced the rest of the room. My arms were around her waist without thinking. Any chance we could get, we were touching each other. I wasn't sure of her motivation, but for me, it was to reassure me that she was alive and well. I'd nearly lost my mind when the bullets started to hit the SUV. We were trapped, and the only thing I could do was place my body on top of hers. With each passing day, our shock wore off and led to anger. We were ready to fight, and whoever got in our way should be scared. We weren't going to take prisoners. It was shoot first, ask questions later. If anyone got in our way or seemed like a threat, their lives would be ended. "While I appreciate that they've let us stay, I want to get the hell out of here and take a shower someplace where I won't come into contact with mold and a myriad of diseases."

And there was no way for me to be deep inside Arely when her brothers were less than ten feet away.

"It shouldn't be too much longer. Last I heard, they were an hour out, and that was forty-five minutes ago. I'd say pack your stuff up if we had anything with us." Santi flashed a smile before he typed something on his phone.

He hadn't left the room the entire time we'd been here. Neither had Arely nor Ale, but it made me wonder if he was here to protect her or for another reason.

Pulling her back to my front, I spoke softly in her ear. "What's wrong?"

She shook her head, and I understood she couldn't talk about it here.

Turning my head to get a better look at her, Arely rested her forehead against my jaw. "I'll tell you later when we're alone."

I nodded as my arms tightened around her.

Santi jumped up, and I could feel his excitement from across the room. We were all ready to get out of this shit hole and seek revenge for the others. It didn't matter that they were guards that I didn't know. They were a part of the organization, and I wouldn't let their lives be canceled out in vain.

"Let's go. We're going out the same way we came

in. Keep your heads down and go to the SUVs I tell you to." I'd barely made a face before he continued. "We're splitting up into more cars. If one car goes down, we all won't fall."

Pablo pushed into Santi and tried to look down on him, but they were the same height, so his intimidation tactic didn't work. "Just tell us our seating arrangements now, or are you afraid we'll fight you?"

"Fine, you're with Army," Santi squared off against his brother. "Bash is with Ale, and I'll be with Arely. Each SUV will have three guards with them, and we'll also have a caravan full of guards in front of and behind us. No one is going to touch us."

I didn't like the idea of not being with Arely, but I understood his tactic.

Santi looked around the room, daring someone to speak. "If you don't like it, then you can stay here because this is how it's going to go down. I'm doing this for everyone's safety."

"I don't like Sebastian not being with me, but I understand your reasoning, and if you think it's best, then I won't complain."

"You heard her. No complaining."

That wasn't what she said, but I wasn't going to argue. I wanted to get the hell out of there.

"Let's go," Santi clapped his hands.

We all stood at once. Taking Arely's hand in mine, I moved toward the door until Santi stopped us. "Say your goodbyes in here. I don't want us out in the open for too long."

Arely turned in my arms and glared at her brother for one second before she twisted back into me. Reaching her hand behind my neck, she pulled me down at the same time she pushed up on her toes. Our lips connected, and a gnawing feeling unleashed itself inside of me. Being apart from Arely was going to be gut-wrenching. I knew I wouldn't be able to take a full breath until she was back by my side.

It wasn't a passionate kiss. It was one of connection. I was surprised when Arely pulled away, and the torment in her eyes matched my own.

Pulling her front to mine, I pressed her cheek into my chest and rested my chin on top of her head. "If you need me, I'm just a phone call away."

"Oh, please, it's not like you're not going to see each other again." The incredulity in his tone let us know he thought we were being ridiculous. "I'll make you a deal. If you ride with me on the way, you can travel with Bash on the way back."

Arely nodded into my chest.

The overwhelming need to tell her I loved her pressed inside my chest. I didn't want the first time I said those words to be with all these people around. I wanted it to be private and only for her.

Even though we'd barely talked the last three days we'd spent holed up in this room, something had grown between us. It was unlike anything I'd ever felt before.

Pushing back, Arely gave me a half-smile. "Let's go." I walked ahead of them with Ale by my side.

"Did they bring guns for everyone?" I heard Arely ask from behind me.

"They brought a whole arsenal," Santi answered her. "What do you want?"

"Nothing big, just a handgun or two. I want to be able to protect myself if I need it." She let out a sigh loud enough for me to hear. "I should have brought my own, but…"

"I know. I had no idea our trip would turn into this." Santi sounded sad and resigned. "I guess we should be thankful we've had as much peace as we have since Father was killed. I've been consulting with others about security. By the time we get back home, no one is going to be able to touch us."

"I hope you're right. I feel like people are coming at us from all sides." Arely's voice shook as she said the last part. I looked over my shoulder at her, but she was looking at the floor as she walked. "We can't let them think they can take us down."

"We won't let them. I promise. Today we have an army with us. Literally. Nothing is going to happen to you."

"I don't want anything to happen to any one of us. I love each and every one of you, and if one of these cowardly assholes took you out, it would wreck me."

"We feel the same way about you. When we get back home, we should go over all the logistics of everything I've set up."

"Yes, we certainly need to talk." The hardness in her voice had me wondering if Santi was what she said we'd talk about later.

I was momentarily blinded when Pablo and Armando opened the door and stepped out into the bright sun. Slipping my sunglasses on, I looked back at Arely one final time before we were separated. With a firm nod, she let me know she was going to be okay.

I watched as she got in the SUV behind us and then as we drove away. Santi wasn't wrong about the army. Behind Arely's SUV was an army truck with a canvas top, the back full of men.

"My sister has you so fucking whipped it's funny. I didn't think you'd be the type," Ale chuckled. He was leaned back in his seat with his eyes closed, acting like someone hadn't tried to kill us just days ago.

Sitting back in my seat, I scanned the area as we

flew through the little town. "She's a special woman. Would you prefer that I cared nothing for her and treated her like shit?"

Peeking one eye open, he took me in and then closed his eye again. "I'm not saying that. While some of the others have a problem with whatever you two have going on, I like seeing my sister happy."

"Life and death situations bring people together. After the other day, I… can't explain it." I wasn't sure her brother needed to know all the ways I felt for his sister. If he knew, he'd probably want to kill me himself.

"I've seen how close you two have become and how you didn't want to be separated. Maybe this short time apart will help you realize what your feelings are."

"I don't need time apart to know how I feel. The only thing I want is to keep her safe." It took everything in me not to look back at her vehicle. "I can't do that from here."

"It might not be the way you want, but if someone comes up, you can shoot at them."

But I couldn't lay my life over hers.

The driver and guard in the front passenger seat spoke rapidly in Spanish, making me once again wish I knew what they were saying.

"Do you speak Spanish?"

"Not much. Why?" I bit out.

Ale smirked. "Because you looked clueless as to what they're saying. You know, you really should learn."

Up until now, I hadn't seen it as a problem. While the Guerrera family spoke in Spanish on occasion, they mainly spoke English, but here, almost every conversation was in Spanish—which was to be expected.

I knew the basics, and that was it. Rapid-fire talking like what was going on in the front seat, I had no idea what was being said. Maybe I should enroll in some Spanish classes at the university next semester.

An hour of complete silence later, the driver spoke. Ale sat up and stretched. "We're almost there."

"Thanks." I looked down at my phone to see no new messages. I wanted to turn around to check to see if Arely was still behind us, but I kept looking forward, flipping my phone on my knee.

"She's fine, you know. She's stronger than all of us combined. If it weren't for her, we'd probably all be living on the streets or worse."

I knew if it weren't for Arely, I wouldn't have been able to move out of my shitty apartment into one that actually had heat in the winter.

"I know not everyone feels this way, or at least they don't want to admit it, but you coming along has been good for her. All she's done for the last few years is work and take care of us. She wouldn't let us do anything for her, but now she's happy when you're around. Or at least when she's not getting shot at."

It felt good to know that Arely let me take care of her when she wouldn't let the others.

The SUV came to a slow roll before stopping on a tree-lined gravel road.

"From here, we walk," Ale announced.

I'd never thought about where this drug lab would be until now, but being out in the middle of nowhere made sense. The only question was how we'd find it.

Stepping out of the SUV, I stretched my legs and watched as Arely and Santi got out of their car. All the men in the trucks lined up along the road. Santi barked out orders, or at least what I thought were orders, since I had no idea what he was saying.

Army and Pablo were fighting until Arely marched up to them and smacked them both in the arms. "You're not helping the cause. Now get your shit together, or you can stay here while we head into the jungle."

Army stood up straight while Pablo slouched against the SUV. Arely circled her finger in the air and started to the tree line.

"Fucking hell, Arely, you can't just go without us," Santi shouted as he ran after her.

I took off after her as well. What was she thinking leaving like that? It wasn't hard to catch up to her, even with her brisk pace.

Santi reached out and put his hand on her shoulder. "Arely, slow down and let everyone catch up. We need you to be safe."

She twirled around with her eyes narrowed. "You don't need to tell me. That's what I heard the entire drive here. When have I done anything unsafe?"

Santi turned back around the way we came with a clenched jaw.

I bit my tongue to keep from saying she'd been unsafe only seconds before. "I don't want to fight with you." I closed my eyes and turned back to the way we'd come. There were footsteps and shouting, but I knew they were from our people, not enemies.

"We're not fighting. I want to get to this damn lab, get some answers, and then get the hell out of here. Is that so hard to understand?"

It wasn't, but it still didn't explain why she ran ahead.

"Do you know your way to the lab?"

"No, but I wasn't going to listen to Santi direct people for half an hour. The ego trip he's on is going to his head." She huffed, crossing her arms over her ample chest.

Wrapping my arm around her shoulders, we stood and waited. I didn't think her brother was on an ego trip. He was trying to keep us all safe. Something had happened on the way here, and she was lashing out, which was so unlike Arely.

A minute later, her brothers and the army they brought with them broke through the trees. I thought there would be yelling, but there was none—just two pissed-off siblings. Santi and our driver from the other day walked past and down a barely discernible path. We got in line and followed behind a group of men in army fatigues who were also carrying guns.

Slipping my arm from around her shoulders, I gripped Arely's hand in mine. I could feel her vibrating, but I didn't know if it was from the ride here, the outcome at the lab, or someone trying to kill her. Or maybe it was all three combined.

We walked for almost forty-five minutes before we stepped into a clearing. There were two long hut-like structures with at least two dozen people working underneath them. The second they saw us, they froze. Terrified eyes stared back at us.

Arely broke away to stand front and center. It was only now I noticed the gun she had slipped into the back of her pants at some point. She spoke in rapid-fire

Spanish, and the workers grew wearier and wearier with each word.

I wished I knew what she was saying. All I knew was that my dick was taking notice, and he liked it. Arely was always hot and assertive, but this was a whole other level. I couldn't wait to get to a hotel and fuck her brains out.

Arely was growling her words now. I assumed no one had admitted to fucking with their product, but then one guy stepped forward and dropped to his knees. He was pleading with her. I really wish I knew what the hell they were saying.

Arely lifted her hand, motioning for the man to rise and come forward. He did so hesitantly as her voice rose. She wasn't shouting. No, Arely was in total control as she spoke. After a few moments, she nodded and then followed the man who'd stepped forward under one of the huts.

I couldn't stay back any longer. I followed her and watched as he showed her around. The working conditions were unfavorable. If the people in the United States could see how hard these people work and how hot and dirty their environment is, maybe they'd complain a little less about their sad jobs.

From what I could gather, one hut was where they made the paste from the leaves, and the other was where they transformed the paste into the actual cocaine. I seriously doubted they had any fentanyl hidden here. It wasn't made here in Colombia, and I doubted they could afford to buy it. Everyone was dressed in dirty clothes that looked as if they'd been worn hard for at least a decade, with holes and tears in them.

Santi stood at the end of one of the huts with his arms crossed over his chest and his eyes drilling into Arely. "Are you ready?"

She nodded, looking around once again. "It's time to go."

We headed back the same way we came, only this time, there was about a foot of space between Arely and me. The trip back didn't seem to take quite as long as the way there. Everyone was quiet except for a few low words spoken here and there.

The second Arely's feet hit the gravel road, she turned and spoke to the army that formed two lines. This time, she didn't sound pissed.

Ale brushed past me, laughing. "You really need to learn Spanish if you're going to stick around."

Arely's head swung around. She looked me up and down, and I swore I could see the disappointment in her eyes that I didn't speak Spanish.

"Let's go," she ordered—her first words in English in over two hours.

"Arely," Santi called to her, but she only held up her hand as she walked toward the SUV she was in earlier.

I slid in beside Arely, watching as everyone loaded up. It wasn't until we started to move that I spoke. "What happened between you and Santi?"

"Brother and sister shit. Nothing you need to worry about," she bit out.

"I'm not worried. If you want to talk about it… you can." I wasn't much for expressing my feelings, and neither was Arely. It was probably one of the reasons why we worked well together. Still, it seemed like it was something more. I knew she and Santi were close, but with each passing day, it seemed as if they were drifting farther and farther away. Something I didn't understand.

"I'm fine. I just want to get to the hotel where I can take a nice, long, hot shower and eat some good food. And then to get out of this country."

Moving closer, I brushed her hair aside and gave her a little nibble on her earlobe. "I can't wait to be alone with you, so I can be deep inside of you and feel you come all over my dick."

Her whole body shuddered, telling me Arely felt the same.

arely

IT FELT like it had been ages since I last hung out with my best friend. We were in the theater room with a blanket covering both our legs, each with our own popcorn bowls on our laps and drinks at our sides. It was just like being at a movie theater, except you didn't have to listen to other people eating or hear them talking or snoring through a movie.

We hadn't picked a movie yet. Instead, Bree and I were catching up on everything that had transpired since the last time we could really talk. The Sunday dinner she attended didn't count.

"I feel like I've hardly seen you since…" she looked down at my stomach where I'd been shot. "And now you've got yourself a boyfriend."

I looked down too, and it was as if I could see

through my clothes. I saw the pink, puckered scar that still twinged every once in a while when I moved a certain way. Everything changed after I got shot.

"I'm sorry. I should have called you back after you left all those voicemails. I was so preoccupied with who shot me that I let a lot of things slide to the wayside."

"You don't need to tell me you're sorry. I can't imagine what you've been going through. Plus, if I know your brothers, they probably wouldn't let you out of their sight."

She wasn't wrong there.

"Only when Sebastian was around would they let me breathe. They hovered over me every second of every day. At one point, I was hoping for a complication just to go back into the hospital, so I could get away from them," I laughed. There was no way I was going back to the hospital, but there were many times I just wanted to be left alone with my thoughts.

"Speaking of Sebastian. He seemed… I guess the word I would use is intense. Which isn't a shocker since he's involved with you," she laughed, and I joined along with her. "But he didn't seem that way with you."

"I don't mind his intensity. It pays off in the bedroom, if you know I mean." I rolled my lips to try and contain my smile, but it was no use. My mouth curved up in a big smile.

Bree clutched her hands to her chest. "I want that."

"Why don't you have it? You're a smoking hot Chinese bombshell. You walk by, and guys jizz in their pants, so what's the problem?" I wasn't lying. Bree was one of the hottest women I'd ever seen. She could easily be a supermodel if she weren't so shy. Her shyness and the fact that she didn't know she was absolutely beautiful only created more allure.

"You think my father will let me date just anyone? They have to go through the inquisition and then some before he'll even grant them one date with me. He scares everyone off before we even have a chance."

Even though her dad was a tiny man, he was scary as shit. He had cold, dead eyes for everyone except Bree.

"Well, I guess we just need to find a guy who can pass the test. Not only with your dad, but with me, too." Bree looked down at the floor and bit her lip. "Unless you already have someone you like."

"Even if I do, he won't be deemed worthy by my father." She looked back up at me and tried to give me a smile, but it was so forced it looked like she was in pain. "Let's get back to you and Sebastian. He looks… younger. How old is he?"

"Oh, he's young, alright. He's definitely not who I would have pictured myself with, but I really like spending time with him even if he is only a sophomore in college."

"A sophomore?" Her brown eyes widened.

"I know. Who would have thought that at thirty, I'd be a cougar?"

"Certainly not me. I thought you might just marry your job and say to hell with men."

"Oh, hell no. I like sex way too much to give up men. Especially Sebastian. He makes me come unlike any other man ever has, and his stamina is otherworldly."

Bree lifted a brow. "Does he have a brother? Maybe I can get a taste knowing my father would never let me date someone so young."

"Unfortunately, he doesn't, but who's to say he didn't have a hot older brother?" I conjured up what I thought Sebastian would look like in ten or twenty years, but I couldn't without seeing what his dad looked like. All I knew was he'd be hot.

Bree started to laugh and fan me with her hand. "You've got it so bad."

"You would be too if he snuck into your bed and had his wicked way with you." I sighed. I couldn't help it after thinking of the way he'd left me feeling boneless while sprawled out on my bed this morning. The man had talent—one I wasn't willing to give up anytime soon.

Bree blushed, and it brought me back to the present. I couldn't help but wonder who it was Bree had a crush on. She was a quiet person but also so damn strong. I knew if she wasn't ready to reveal who she liked, she wouldn't.

Grabbing her hand in mine, I gave it a slight squeeze. "We need to do this more often. I missed you, and you know you are always invited to Sunday dinner."

"Maybe I'll stay tonight then. It's better than eating dinner with my family. I'm not sure why my father requires us all to eat together if we can't speak during dinner. Eating dinner with you is always so lively."

That was a good way to put it. My brothers were always entertaining. I couldn't remember the last time I'd eaten dinner at Bree's. It felt like everyone was just sitting around watching you eat, waiting for someone to speak when they knew it would never happen.

"Of course, you can stay. I'm not done with you yet. We haven't even watched our movie or eaten our popcorn."

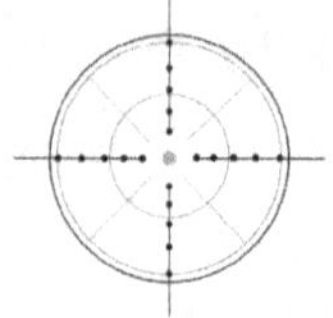

Standing at my bedroom window, instead of seeing the lake behind my house, all I saw were guards walking the perimeter with guns on their backs. This was my life now. It wasn't quiet, and I couldn't leave at a moment's notice. I had a whole brigade of men who went everywhere I did. Good luck to anyone who tried to take me out now.

I was shocked to find Pablo standing just inside my door when I stepped into my bedroom from my office. "I didn't expect to see you here. Is everything okay?"

Stepping forward, he moved to my side and placed my hand in the crook of his elbow. This wasn't the norm for us. "Perfectly fine. I thought I'd walk you down since Santi is talking with Bree, and Bash isn't here yet."

I cocked my head in his direction to find my oldest brother with a slight curve of his lips. "Do you have a girlfriend I don't know about?" I asked, wondering if this was why he was acting the way he was.

For the briefest of seconds, he paused but then kept going. "How did you know?"

"You seem happier." It was the only explanation. "You know, if you want, you can invite her to dinner."

"I know, but it's new yet. I don't want the lot of you to scare her off. When the time is right, I'll introduce her to all of you."

"Do you really think we would scare her?" I laughed. It would be fun to try and chase off Army's fake little girlfriend, but I knew the task wasn't easy since this was her job. I wasn't sure how he kept her in his company, knowing who she was.

Pablo lifted a brow. "Hell, yes, you would. Why do you think I keep my love life away from this house?"

He wasn't wrong. Our dynamic could be a lot to take in. Still, I hated the thought that he felt like he couldn't share that part of his life with us.

"If you ask, we'll try to behave."

"Don't worry about it." He smiled. "When the time is right, you'll meet her. I was surprised to find Bash wasn't back yet."

Today was the first day Sebastian had left my side since we'd gotten back from Colombia last week. He was practically living here. When I told him he could leave a few things here, I should have just asked him to move in. It wasn't like he would be bringing his furniture with him.

"Where did he go off to?"

"I didn't ask." I didn't feel the need, and if I wanted to, I could call him if I needed him, which I didn't.

We reached the bottom of the stairs. Pablo patted my hand wrapped around his arm. "Do you trust him one hundred percent?"

"Yes. I have no doubts about him." Stepping away, I looked him up and down, trying to understand why he had asked. "How can you? He's saved me and put his body before mine to keep me safe."

"I don't know. It could all be fake. With each step, he's worming his way into our family and business, and the closer he gets, the more bad shit happens. What if he's working for someone to take us all out?"

"While you have reason to be paranoid, it isn't Sebastian. He didn't send himself the test to kill me. He's not a part of the society yet. You weren't there all the times he's saved me."

"You almost died when you were shot. I don't call that good saving. Just… be careful. He might not be who he says he is." He held up his hands as I narrowed my eyes at him. I didn't understand why this was coming up now. "Don't get me wrong. I like the guy. I do, but now isn't the time to let down your guard."

"Santi did his background check on Sebastian. If there was anything to find, he would have."

"Right, Santiago, who left you at the church

unattended? He was your one bodyguard. Why would he leave you unprotected? Has it ever occurred to you that he's the only one who knew where you were?"

Yes, it had, but I wasn't going to tell him that. I didn't like where this conversation was going.

"Have you asked these questions to Santi?" I turned and headed in the direction of the dining room. "If not, you can bring them up at our meeting after dinner."

"Maybe I will." He quirked a brow, challenging me.

Before I could throw a comeback at him, Sebastian came through the door, clutching his side. The clothes he left in earlier were dirty and torn.

Running over, I wrapped my arm around his waist as he started to list to the side. "What the hell happened?"

"Some asshole stabbed me when I was leaving my apartment." He winced when his side came into contact with mine.

As he spoke the words, I felt the cold wetness on his side. My eyes scanned to find where he'd been injured.

"And you came here, why?" Pablo sneered.

Looking up from trying to find the wound, I found Pablo looking at us with disgust. "What the fuck is wrong with you? Go get the others," I barked out.

Slowly, I moved Sebastian over into the sitting room and down onto one of the couches.

Sitting down beside him, I lifted his shirt to find a stab wound to the right side of his ribs that was sluggishly pouring out blood. "Don't worry. We'll get you patched up. Santi knows someone who can help. Believe it or not, but this isn't a regular thing around here."

Our eyes met, and he frowned. "Was it wrong of me to come here? What if I led them right where they want to be?"

"No, you did the right thing. If this is retaliation for the Guerrera Syndicate, they might have tried to finish the job at the hospital."

Leaning forward, he pressed his forehead to mine. I was surprised he was so calm and subdued. "I'm just glad it wasn't you this time."

"I'm sorry this happened because of me. I tried to give you an out before it was too late." But now everyone knew Sebastian was a part of us and if they knew that, they probably surmised he was special to me. The worst possible position to be in.

"Arely, I'll be fine." Slowly, he brought his warm palm up to cup the side of my face. He stared at me for a long minute as if he was looking into my soul. "I'd gladly get stabbed a thousand times over to prevent you an ounce of pain."

A loud throat clearing broke us apart before Santi spoke. "Alright, if you two lovebirds could break apart, I'd like to take a look at the wound."

Reluctantly, I stood to give him the room he needed, even though I didn't want to leave Sebastian's side. Needing to be close to him, I rounded the back of the couch and placed my hands on Sebastian's shoulders.

"While I could staple this up, I'm going to call the doctor to make sure no organs were hit, or it isn't more serious."

"More serious than an organ being hit?" Sebastian laughed weakly.

Santi stood from inspecting the wound, his eyes landing on me. "How about we take him to the guest room down here until the doctor arrives?"

"Fine, help me get him up." I wanted Sebastian in my bedroom, but I wasn't going to put him through going up the stairs for my wants. Being downstairs would be easier for everyone involved, and I really didn't want the doctor to know where my bedroom was either. With each passing day, I learned not to trust many people.

How had it gotten to the point where I wasn't sure

if I could trust my brother and very best friend in the whole world but could trust Sebastian, who was only twenty years old, and I'd only known him for a few short months? Was I being naïve and letting my feelings blind me? I didn't think so. My gut was always right, and it told me I could trust Sebastian. It also told me that he was true to me and only me with all of the evidence that was starting to stack up against Santi.

Even if that was the case, I had to watch out for someone out there who wasn't on our side.

Santi and Ale helped Sebastian to the only guest room we had on the first floor. He didn't protest until they tried to help him lie down.

"I've got it," he pushed them away. "I'm not a total invalid, and I don't think I'm going to die anytime soon."

"Fine, bro, I was just trying to help." Ale stepped back. "If you need me, I'm just a call away. What should we do about dinner? Everyone's been waiting—"

"Go on with dinner. There won't be a meeting tonight." I waved them away.

"Arely, you don't have to do that for me. I'm fine by myself until the doctor gets here." He winced as he went to lie down, and that was all I needed to stay. Not that I planned on leaving him, anyway.

"I'm staying, and that's final." I moved to sit on the bed beside him. "You guys go eat and let Bree know I'll call her later."

"Like Ale said, we're just a call away. I'll be back once the doctor gets here. It wasn't life or death, so it may be a while."

"For what I pay that man, he should be chartering a helicopter to get here as fast as he can, but whatever. Leave us until he gets here," I ordered.

I kept my eyes on my brothers until the bedroom door was shut, and I heard them walk away. I moved closer to Sebastian, lifting his shirt to see if the bleeding had slowed down. It hadn't. It was flowing more than when I looked at it before. It was probably from Sebastian moving around.

"I'll be right back," I said, looking over my shoulder as I went to the en suite bathroom and ripped the hand towel from where it hung on the wall. "I should have done this sooner, but I think I was in shock." I climbed back onto the bed and pressed the towel to where he was bleeding.

He closed his eyes and looked strangely peaceful for someone who'd just been stabbed.

"Does it hurt?"

"Like a bitch, but I can handle it. I'm sure it's

nothing compared to being shot." His left eye popped open and fixed on me.

"You have no idea who it was who stabbed you?"

"None. I haven't seen him before." He closed his eye and reached for my hand at the same time. "It might not be related to you. I mean, not directly. It could be I sold him drugs at one point and thought he could kill me and steal the drugs and money."

"Did he rob you?"

"Fuck no. I fought back. He's probably more injured than me after I slammed my fist into his face a few times. I doubt he'll be coming back for more."

"I don't want to risk the chance. You have enough of your stuff here. You'll stay. I can send a few guards to your house to gather the rest of your belongings." Blood started to seep through the towel, making me press harder.

Turning his head, Sebastian opened both eyes and looked at me. His light brown eyes held pain in them, but something else I couldn't recognize. "Is that your way of asking me to move in?"

"No, this is me telling you you're moving in. I'm not going to risk you getting hurt again." I brushed a strand of hair off his forehead and ran my fingers over his brows and cheekbones.

"If you want me to stay, you need to talk to me. You

said you were going to tell me what's going on with you and Santi in Colombia, but you haven't said a word to me."

My whole body deflated. "Because I don't like to think about the possibility that he might have betrayed me."

"What?" His brows puckered. "How could you think that?"

"It's not just me. Pablo even suggested it might be Santiago before you got here." I took in a deep breath and held it for as long as I could. When I exhaled, I was only filled with sadness. "He's the only one who knew where I was, and he left me there for a hookup, which he shouldn't have done as my head of security."

His face relaxed as he asked. "What's at that church?"

"That's where I used to do most of my work. Who's going to suspect that a drug ring is being run in the secret bowels of a church?"

"Not many," he frowned and paused. "You're right, but don't all of your brothers know of the church?"

"They do, but it's not their job to protect me." I leaned my head back against the headboard and let out a defeated sigh. "The only person who knew I'd be there that late was Santi. Even though I don't want to believe it, all indications are pointing straight at him."

"I can't believe it either. Pablo, yes, but not Santi. Hell, I can't imagine Ale or Army turning their backs on you."

"Neither can I," I faced toward the bedroom door and thought of my family, who were eating dinner as we spoke. "But it's looking as if someone did. The question is who."

"Are you going to fire me now?"

His question was so far off-topic and out of the blue. I swung my gaze back to look at him. "What are you talking about?"

"I got stabbed, and I wasn't even protecting you when it happened. All I did was walk out of my apartment building," he laughed bitterly.

Sliding down on the bed, I cupped the side of his face. The scruff on his jaw prickled underneath my fingertips. "I'm not firing you unless you feel like you're no longer up for the job."

His gaze never wavered as he spoke. "I never want to leave you. I'll fight for you until my last breath."

Leaning forward until my mouth was close enough to brush against his, I spoke from the heart. Each word breathed life into what was happening between us as my lips grazed his. "Good. I don't want you to ever let me go."

Pressing forward, Sebastian removed any space that

was left between us. Our mouths locked together, tongues dancing and caressing in a sensual dance. I moaned into his mouth as I tangled my fingers in his hair to deepen the kiss.

A loud knock broke us apart, and a second later, Santi and the doctor stepped into the room.

Doctor Phillipstein was in his late sixties with white hair and wrinkles that showed he'd lived a good life. He was tall and wiry and moved with grace not many had as they aged.

"Alright, young man, let's see the damage and get you patched up." The doctor lifted up the towel and inspected the wound. "Why don't the two of you leave us, and I'll come get you when we're done?"

I looked at Sebastian to see if he wanted me here, but he nodded, letting me know he was fine.

With Sebastian being treated, it was now time to do something I never thought I'd have to do.

arely

STEPPING out of the guest bedroom, I made a right. "Where's everyone else?"

Santi came into step with me as we walked down the hall and out into the backyard by the pool. It was already dark, but the area was lit with lights and the glow from the pool. "Finishing dinner. Why? Did you want me to get them?"

"No, I want to talk to you and only you, my best friend." I rounded on him. "I need answers, and I need them now before anyone else gets hurt."

He stepped back and then moved to sit down on one of the outdoor couches. "I don't know who hurt Bash. Not yet, anyway."

"You still haven't figured out who tried to kill me or all of us." I stood in front of him, not willing to get comfortable. This wasn't that type of conversation. "The one thing I can't put my finger on is how whoever sent Sebastian to kill me knew I'd be at the church. Only our family knows about it."

"Anyone could follow you, Arely. It wouldn't have been hard. I'm not saying they would know the base of our operations were there. They could think you're highly religious and going there to pray or confess."

"Okay, I'll give you that, but whoever it was would also have to know about the Scorpio Society and be able to get their hands on the parchment they write out the tests on."

"You don't think I know that," he shouted. "Every time I think about it, I get sick to my stomach knowing I left you there unprotected. And now, now," he raised his voice even louder. "You've got your boyfriend watching out for you."

"Shouldn't any good boyfriend or girlfriend watch out for you?" I raised my brows, waiting for his response.

"Yes, but they normally aren't protecting them from harm and death on a daily basis. You replaced me with *him*. How do you think it makes me feel?"

"And how do you think it makes me feel that my own brother and best friend might have tried to kill me?"

Santi's eyes widened into saucers as he stared up at me. His face was slack-jawed in utter shock. "You seriously think it was me?"

"My heart doesn't want to believe it, but all clues lead back to you, and it's not only me who thinks so."

He jumped up and started to pace in front of the couch. "Oh, your boyfriend who tried to kill you is blaming me," he scoffed.

"Actually, he doesn't. And he didn't try to kill me. There's a difference between being sent to do the deed and attempting it. Once he saw it was me, he dropped his knife."

Stopping in front of me, he crossed his arms over his chest and widened his stance. "Oh, the same knife that stabbed him today?"

"Do you really believe he stabbed himself?" I laughed darkly, not believing his accusation in the slightest.

"You believe I could put a hit on you?"

"Santi," I sighed and moved toward him. Gripping his biceps, I looked into his dark, troubled eyes. "I don't want to, but what would you have me believe when all signs point in your direction?"

He spread his arms wide and looked down at me with devastation written across his stricken face.

"Believe that as your brother and best friend, I would never do anything to harm you."

"You can't deny that you're hiding something from me." I shook his arms where I held him. "Tell me what it is, and I'll forget about the other."

"I can't do that. It's not only my secret to tell," he shook his head. Sadness swirled in the depths of his eyes as he implored me to believe him. "You know in your heart it's not me. If anything, I'm being framed. What better way to get to you than to eliminate the people who are protecting you? Set it up to look like it's me, and then kill off your boyfriend."

What he said made sense, but how could I believe anything else without proof?

"Why would I want to kill you and build an army to protect you? It doesn't make sense. Trust your gut, Arely. I love you more than anyone else on this planet, and to know that you think I might hurt you wounds me deeply. It feels like I'm the one who was stabbed." Tears swelled in his eyes, and I did the only thing I could. I pulled my brother into my arms and hugged him as tightly as I possibly could.

"I love you, Santi, but I don't like that you're hiding something from me. You and I don't keep secrets from each other."

"I know," he choked out. "It won't hurt you but

someone else if I tell this secret. Trust me to know I'm doing what's best for all of us," he spoke into the crown of my head.

I nodded, knowing all I could do was trust my gut in this moment. It was too difficult to bear the thought of my brother betraying me.

Pulling out of his embrace, I smiled sadly. When had we gotten this way?

"Are you keeping this from me because you hate Sebastian?"

"I don't hate him. In fact, I like that he's made you happy. For so long, you only lived for work. While we all appreciate the world you've built for us, making our business more profitable than Father ever did, you've taken too much of it on your shoulders. We are all here to help you. Don't you think Ale and Army would be more useful than working on the streets?"

"Of course I do, but I want them to go to school—something we didn't have the opportunity to do—and enjoy it. What if they don't want to be a part of this life? I want them to have options."

Santi's mouth cracked into a smile. "They're not going anywhere, but I'm sure their business knowledge will help us in the future. They'll be able to make our legitimate businesses more profitable. The point is to enjoy your life and put more on our shoulders. You can start small, but we all want to help you more."

He was right. It was time to make it more of a family operation than an Arely one. I had taken on the brunt of the work for too long.

"I will." I looked back to the house, wondering if the doctor was done with Sebastian yet. "Since we're not having a meeting, any news on the fake girlfriend?"

"No, she's keeping her head down, and from what I know, isn't pushing when Army keeps her in the dark about what he's doing. This would be the best time to have him stop selling and do something else that can't be traced back to him while she's on our tail. We have to make sure she doesn't learn anything."

"This is why I keep you around. You have all the good ideas." I hugged him one more time before I looked back at the house once again.

"Get back to Sebastian. I know it's killing you to be away from him. Do you…" he stopped and then shook his head.

"Do I, what? Ask me, Santi. Anything."

"Do you love him?" He quietly asked as if the question pained him. I didn't understand why it was so hard for him to ask such a simple question.

"I think I do, but I haven't said it to him or anything."

"Why not? You're certainly not shy and always go after what you want."

No, I wasn't. I knew that when I went back in there and saw Sebastian again, I would tell him how I felt. And maybe, just maybe, he'd feel the same.

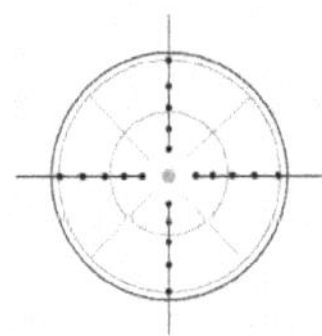

STEPPING INSIDE THE GUEST BEDROOM, I found Sebastian sprawled out on the bed with a bandage over his wound.

"Why do you look scared? I'm fine." He gave me a tip of his lips. "The doctor said I'll be as good as new in a couple of weeks as long as I don't tear the stitches out."

"We'll have to keep you in bed to make sure that doesn't happen." I moved toward the side of the bed he was lying on before sitting down.

"If you're anywhere near me in that bed, it's a surefire way for me to rip at least a couple."

I patted his chest just above his heart. "I'll try to be gentle with you, then. I'd hate to be the cause for your recovery time to be extended."

"I wouldn't mind," he smiled drowsily. It wasn't until then I noticed how tired he looked.

"How are you feeling? Did the doctor give you some drugs?"

"The best fucking drugs. I can't feel a thing." He wrapped his arm around my waist and pulled me close to him. "I'm tired, though."

"I bet. How about you get some sleep, and when you wake up, we'll eat some of the dinner we missed?"

"Shit, I'm sorry, I fucked up dinner. Did you at least have your meeting?" His eyes drooped and then popped back open.

"No meeting, but I did talk to Santi while the doctor was in here with you."

"That must have been a long talk. I think the doctor was in here for at least an hour, and then I took a nap." There was a long blink, and then his eyes landed on mine.

"It wasn't that long at all. I think it's the drugs." Tracing my fingers over his forehead, brows, and then his eyes, I held them there for a moment before I ran my fingers through the strands of his hair, trying to lull him to sleep.

Once I knew he was asleep, I slowly got up and left the room. I had no idea how long he'd sleep, but I figured it would be at least an hour or two.

I moved through my quiet house, surprised by the silence but happy for it nonetheless after the day I'd had. I slipped out into the backyard, knowing I'd find at least one guard who could help me. I was almost to the lake before I felt a presence behind me. They weren't supposed to interrupt me unless I was in danger.

Spinning on my heels, I turned to find a man standing in the dark. I couldn't make out who it was, but I knew it was one of my guys. Santi and Javier had hired so many men I had no idea what their names were.

"I need you to round up a team to head to Sebastian's house and pack up all of his personal items. Leave the furniture and don't make a mess out of his place. Once you have everything here, I want you to put it in the hall outside of my bedroom. Do not step inside my room under any circumstances. Do you understand?"

"Yes, Ms. Guerrera," he bowed his head. "I'll get on it right away." He turned and disappeared into the night just as quickly as he appeared.

Even though it was too cold to sit outside without a jacket or a blanket, I made my way down to the dock. I sat at the end with my feet hanging off, looking out at the dark water before me. It was peaceful here and was one of the reasons I bought the house. That and the fact there were enough rooms for everyone and more. I liked keeping my family close, and having them all under one roof was one way we stayed that way.

Boots hitting the wooden planks alerted me to someone coming up from behind me before he spoke. "I thought I'd find you here," Ale said as he sat down beside me. "How's Bash?"

"Sleeping peacefully. Dr. Phillipstein gave him the good shit. I sent some of the guards to get the rest of his things. He's going to stay here from now on."

"Arely," he chuckled. "Bash was already living here. The only difference was he didn't have all of his things here. Don't wait for everyone's approval. Do what makes you happy, even if that is Bash." He laughed harder at his own joke.

"I don't care what anyone else thinks. If they have a problem, tough shit. I'm not going to let Sebastian get hurt because of us again." Looking out into the darkness, I watched as each attack played out before my eyes. It was too much and happening far too often. "If someone hurts one of us, we end whoever it was slowly and painfully."

"I agree. When you first brought on all the guards, I thought it might have been an overreaction, but now… shit, it's like we need a posse with each of us wherever we go to protect our backs."

"Maybe we lie low for a while and let the street guys do the selling. We need to change up how we do everything. Once we have a new plan in place, we emerge stronger than ever and let them know they can't touch us. If they try, they die."

Out of the corner of my eye, I saw him nodding. "While I don't like hiding, I do think we need a new structure for how we do things. We need to make sure everyone is on the same page."

"We'll have a meeting tomorrow, but let the others know I don't want anyone leaving until after we all talk." I started to stand. Ale stood first and held his hand out to me. I took it, letting him help me to my feet before I gave him a short hug. "I'll see you tomorrow."

"Get some rest."

I wasn't sure how easy that was going to be.

We walked back to the house in silence. Everything was so easy with Ale. He was the strong, silent type who never spoke unless it was important. Well, unless he was with Army, then he was relaxed and carefree. I wanted him to be that way all the time. I knew it was hard for him to be gay in the world we lived in. He knew our family would support him no matter who he chose to spend his life with.

Before heading up to see if Sebastian's things had been delivered, I peeked in to find him still passed out in the exact same position I left him. Only for a moment did I think about joining before I closed the door and made my way upstairs to my bedroom. Along the wall, I found a pile of clothes still on their hangers and a large duffle bag packed to the brim, along with Sebastian's backpack. I felt my mouth turn down as I realized this was all of Sebastian's personal belongings. He barely had anything to his name. Maybe I should have gone to his apartment to see how he lived and to understand him better.

Back and forth, I went about unpacking his belongings to mingle with my own. I thought I might have to make room and get rid of a few things or put them in another closet. Instead, after all of his clothes were hung up in the space I'd designated for him, it still looked sparse. Even the drawers on his side of the bathroom barely had anything in them.

This was something I could rectify.

Grabbing my laptop out of my office, I headed back down to the guest room to find Sebastian still sleeping. I was starting to get hungry now that the adrenaline from earlier had worn off. However, I had promised Sebastian we would eat together. Crawling up on the bed beside him, I sat with my laptop and pulled up a few websites where I usually shopped for my brothers. An hour later, and almost a thousand dollars spent on clothes, Sebastian started to stir.

Turning on his side toward me, he wrapped his hand around my forearm and gave me a sleepy smile. "Have you been here the entire time?"

"I couldn't just sit here and listen to your snore the entire time."

The corner of his mouth tipped up. "I don't snore."

"How would you know? You're sleeping," I chuckled.

Sebastian moved closer to me, snuggling into my side. He was quite affectionate when he was sleepy and drugged. "I've never had anyone complain before."

He must have still been seriously drugged if he thought I wanted to hear about all the women who hadn't complained. Snapping my laptop closed, I slid off the bed and started for the door. "Now that you're awake, I'm going to get something to eat. You're welcome to join me if you'd like."

He was still where I left him, with his brows knitted together. "I'd like to take a quick shower and clean up, if that's alright with you?"

"You don't have to ask my permission. This is your house too."

I barely had the door open when he spoke again. "I

thought that was a dream. Do you really want me here?"

"Your things are already hanging in my closet upstairs. Come join me when you're done." I slipped out the door and made my way to the kitchen. Maybe I should've put his things in one of the guest bedrooms, but no, I wasn't going to play games. Just because he said something stupid, I wasn't going to throw him out of my bed.

We had voted for Italian tonight. I put the lasagna in the oven and went about making some new garlic bread to eat with it. Pulling out the salad, I set it on the island. There had been more, so much more, but my brothers had eaten it all. I swear they didn't eat all week in preparation for Sunday night dinner—which I knew wasn't true because most of the time, they stayed here, and there was always food. The only ones who didn't live here full-time were the twins, which gave them the full college experience.

"It smells good. I'm sorry we missed it the first time around." Sebastian ambled into the room and sat at the island across from me. His hair was still damp. He'd changed into a pair of gray sweatpants and a bright white t-shirt that stretched across his chest.

"I don't think you intended to get stabbed, so it's quite alright. The lasagna should only be another few minutes. Do you want to start with a salad?" I started to plate myself some when he reached across the space and took my hand.

I met his turbulent brown eyes and set down the serving tongs. "You didn't have to move my things here or hang them up. I'm perfectly capable of doing those things for myself."

"Perhaps, but we're on lockdown until we have a meeting tomorrow to figure out a new structure. You should have had protection with you." His jaw ticked, but I continued. "If you didn't want to take your guy, you should have at least had a gun on you."

"I didn't think I needed it since you weren't with me, but now I see the error in my ways." He looked down at his side.

"I gave you an out before."

"And I didn't take it. I'm never going to take it." His usual light brown eyes darkened as he stared at me.

"It's too late to get out unless you want to relocate. You're in, and everyone knows about you."

"How?"

"Do you not realize people are surveilling us to find kinks in our armor when we're out? You've been seen by my side too many times. You're associated with me, either as my guard, and the quickest way to get to me is to take you out, or as my lover and hopefully my weakness."

His throat bobbed before he spoke. His hand gripping mine tighter. "I don't want to be your weakness."

"Too late. Each and every one of you is my weakness. I would go through Hell to get any of you back."

Before I could say more or read his expression, the timer on the oven went off, signaling the lasagna was done. Stepping back, I pulled it out and set it on the counter beside the garlic bread. I put a serving on each of our plates and stood across from Sebastian as I ate. He may not have been hungry since he was drugged, but I was hungry before he showed up bleeding. Once the adrenaline of the night wore off, I became tired and ravenous. I was halfway through my meal when he cleared his throat. I looked up from my plate to find him standing and coming around to stand in front of me.

"Do you not like the food?"

"The food is fine," he muttered as he wrapped his arms around my middle and pressed me tight into his body.

I chanced a glance over to see he'd barely touched his dinner. "What's wrong?"

"Nothing's wrong. I just wanted to feel you in my arms." He dipped down a brushed a minty kiss on my lips.

Wrapping my arms around his torso, I buried my face in his chest and breathed him in. "I like being in your arms."

"I've been wanting to tell you something since we were in Colombia, but I've been holding back, waiting for the right time."

I could hear his heart start to beat faster and faster with each passing second. Pulling back, I looked up at him to find Sebastian's face pale. Was he going to end us?

He knew too much, and if he wanted entirely out of our lives, there was only one way to do that, and I really didn't want to have to end his life.

"The time we spent together in Colombia, even though we didn't have a moment alone, made me realize my feelings for you."

That he had none? No, that couldn't be right unless he wanted to get his rocks off a few more times before he ended things.

"Who would have ever thought that me trying to steal your purse would bring us to this moment?" He chuckled nervously. "I sure didn't, but I've never been happier to get caught." He rubbed his thumb over my bottom lip and pressed against the flesh. "I love you, Arely, and with each passing day, it's been harder and harder to keep those words inside. I needed you to know how I feel about you. It's okay if you don't feel the same way."

And here I was thinking about how I'd hate to kill him.

Cupping the sides of his face with both of my hands, I pulled him down until his forehead met mine. "How could you think I don't feel the same? I never thought I'd find someone I wanted to keep forever, but I have. You're it for me, Sebastian King."

Gripping my hips, he pulled me tighter against his body, letting me feel his hard length against my thigh. His eyes lit up, and I knew I was in for the most delicious night of my life. "What do you say we ditch the food down here, and I eat you upstairs?

bash

SITTING IN THE SUV, I watched as one of our dealers flipped through his money and then pocketed a sizable portion in one pocket and stuffed the other down his pants. I guess he thought we wouldn't deep dive into his underwear to look for the money he was stealing.

Stepping out of the car, I walked silently, not letting him know I was coming until the last minute. He didn't hear me until it was too late, and my forearm was wrapped around his neck, applying pressure. He struggled, but I didn't let him go. Instead, I nodded toward the car. It pulled up in front of us, and the back popped open. I threw the dealer into the back and tied his arms and legs together before hopping into the backseat. Twisting around, I sneered at him.

"Did you really think we wouldn't figure out you've been stealing from us for the last month?"

"I had to. My girl just had a baby, and those things are expensive as hell," he shouted back like he was in the right.

"That still doesn't give you the right. What's your girl going to do now when you don't come back?"

"No, you wouldn't do that." He paled. "You can't. I have valuable information about who's been trying to take out the Guerrera's. I pr—promise to tell you everything I know if you let me live."

"Unfortunately, that's not for me to decide. I hope for your sake that you're telling the truth because if not, you're going to wish I'd killed you now."

I turned around and watched the scenery go by as we made our way back to the estate. It didn't take us long to pull up outside the house. Grabbing the dealer by his bound hands, I shuffled him inside the house, down the first flight of stairs to the basement, and then down to the dungeon. I hadn't seen anyone else brought here since I'd been locked away in it, but it still smelled like blood and piss—a combination that would set off anyone's gag reflex. Along the way, I passed Pablo, who looked on with curiosity.

"Who do you got there?"

"A dealer who's been stealing. He says he has

important information to give up. I'm going to lock him up and then get everyone before interrogating him."

Pablo gripped the guy's arm. "I'll take him while you get the others."

"Are you sure? I can do both." It was rare that Pablo spoke to me, so I was shocked he offered to help me. He was part of the business side, not the muscle.

"Yeah, Arely is up in her office with Santi."

The dealer tried to jerk away from Pablo with no success. I elbowed him in the ribs, causing him to groan and clutch at his side. He looked up at me with terrified eyes. I wasn't sure what had changed since being in the car. He knew if he lied to us or his information was shit, he was forfeiting his life.

"Thanks." I turned on my heel and took the stairs three at a time until I reached the floor with Arely's office. The door was closed as per usual. I knocked lightly on the door before I opened it. Arely sat behind her desk with a scowl on her face.

I moved to stand beside her desk. "I have someone downstairs that says he knows who's been trying to take you out."

They both jumped up at the same time. "Where did you find him?" She asked.

"I told you I was close to figuring out who was stealing from you. I caught him in the act. When I threw him in the back of the car, he begged for his life."

"And you think he's being truthful?" Santi raised a brow at me and gave me a look that said I was naïve.

"I'm not sure, but I wanted to make sure we at least tried to get the information out of him."

"Good job. Even if he doesn't know, we have to make him an example."

I knew that. However, I wasn't sure if they'd expect me to kill the guy or not.

We hit the bottom floor and found Pablo walking out of the one of the rooms with blood all over his face and shirt.

"What the hell happened to you?" Santi asked, looking his brother over.

"He tried to escape, and I had to shoot him." Pablo brushed by us like it was any other day and not that he just informed us he'd killed the one lead we'd had in months.

Santi stalked toward the cell. He peered inside, and when he looked back at his sister, he shook his head.

Arely flew up the stairs after Pablo.

How could that guy have tried to get away? His hands and feet were bound, and who cared if he tried to run? He wasn't a threat with his hands behind his back.

Stepping into the room, I found the dealer in a pool of his own blood. He wasn't tied up anymore, but I didn't understand why Pablo would have untied him.

"Help me get him out to the pig stye," Santi demanded.

Grabbing the guy's legs, I lifted at the same time as Santi. "The what?"

"Pigs. They're great at making evidence… disappear," he smirked.

I guess when they mentioned pigs all those months ago, they weren't lying.

We climbed the stairs, Santi holding the dealer's upper body as he traversed backward while I held his legs.

"I don't understand why he tried to escape. If he had good intel, he might have been let go."

"Fight or flight instinct. When he saw where we were putting him, rational thought left him." He raised his head to look at me. "It's happened before."

I wasn't sure what that said about me that I let them hold me down here for days without thinking of trying to escape.

"You know, you surprised us when you didn't fight."

"I knew I was innocent," I shot back. Mostly my thoughts had been on Arely and if she would make it.

Beyond that, I hardly thought of anything else when I was held. "Just like you."

His jaw hardened. "It's fucked up. Someone is trying to frame me. I would…" his throat bobbed as he stared down at me. "I would never hurt Arely, let alone attempt to kill her. This whole thing is fucked up. We've never been under siege like this before."

"Everyone wants what you have. I guess you should be flattered." I chuckled darkly.

"If I'd had all of our security set up like it is now after our father was killed, none of this would have happened. We were all too young and dumb to realize what we were getting into at the time. It doesn't help, but I thought being a part of the Scorpio Society brought us a level of protection that obviously is not there."

One of the guards opened the door for us, and we stepped out into the cool night air.

"You know now, and that's all that matters." I looked around, wondering where these pigs were as I followed Santi into the garage.

"Let's put him in there," he nodded toward a side-by-side. "We'll drive back." Putting the body on an attached trailer, we got into the utility vehicle, and Santi drove off into the dark. "I guess Arely didn't share the location of our pets."

"No, she didn't." Not that I cared.

"She's not used to opening up to others outside her family. It might take her some time to… learn."

I wasn't going to tell Santi that his sister told me more than he knew. He obviously knew she'd told me about her suspicions about him.

After a few minutes, we pulled up to a barn that I'd never seen before. You couldn't even see it from the house. It made me wonder just how much land they owned. Once the motor cut off, I could hear the squeal of pigs. I'd never been around pigs before, so I was unsure what to expect. I stood back in surprise when three large pigs ran over to Santi for him to pet them.

"Are they usually so… affectionate?" I wasn't sure that was the right word to describe them, but they did want attention and some rubs.

He nodded toward the side-by-side, and I followed him. "I think I'm the only person who comes out here to visit them except for the groundskeeper. He tends to the area and feeds them."

"And what? We just throw this to them, and they…"

"Eat the body," Santi finished for me. "It's not something you want to stick around for. First, help me strip him."

You'd think it was easy to strip a dead guy, but that

was far from the truth. His body was stiff, making it difficult to remove each item. After trying unsuccessfully to get his leg out of his jeans, I pulled out my knife.

"Ah, I was wondering how long it would take you." He was grinning down at me as I hunched over the body and cut the clothes away. "You're smart for a young guy."

"Does my age bother you?" I grunted as I rolled the body to the side to pull the clothes out from under him.

"It's never been your age. It's you." He shook his head when I narrowed my eyes at him. "It could have been anyone. I'm not used to having to share Arely with anyone but my family, and even then, I was top priority."

"And you feel that now you aren't? I can attest that your sister loves you very much." I didn't want to betray Arely, but I felt if I spoke to what I could, it might help their relationship. I could do that for her even if I didn't give a shit about her brother. "You need to spend more time with your sister, not less. Remind her of the love you share and how much she means to you."

"Oh, and I'm supposed to do that while you're glued to my sister?" He sneered, his face twisted up in rage.

"I'm happy to give you alone time with her." Why couldn't he spend time with her while I was at school? I wasn't sure. The twins and I were back in class with our own army surrounding us in the shadows of the university.

"I'm not sure she wants to spend time with only me. Her trust in me is shaky at best."

"And you think distancing yourself is helping matters? It's not. Ask her to lunch one day while I'm gone to class. Do something except let more time and space separate you."

He huffed. "You know my sister well, it seems." He clapped his hands together. "Enough of this talk. Help me carry him over to the pen."

I guess our talk was over. I helped Santi pick up and throw the body over the side of the pen and watched in horror and fascination as the pigs ran to the body and started in on their job. The sounds of flesh ripping and teeth scraping against bones wasn't a sound I would soon forget.

If things between Arely and I didn't work out for some reason, I wondered if I would be dragged out here for the pigs to eat?

bash

I COULD FEEL ARELY'S eyes on me as she watched me dress. She wasn't happy that the day after someone claimed they had information that would help us, the Scorpio Society decided it was finally time to give me my test.

"Ale and Army could follow behind to make sure—"

"You know they can't do that. I have to go alone in case anyone is watching." I turned to look at her standing at the mouth of the closet. "If I don't pass, will I really die?"

"Not necessarily, but let's not take that chance. You're going to pass whatever test it is they have for you, and then you're going to come home to me. Are we clear?"

It was hot that she was so worried about me.

"I'll send you a text the second I'm finished." I hadn't even read what it was they wanted me to do yet. All I'd done was inform Arely that I'd received my second test and I'd be back later. As soon as I saw it sitting on the driver's side seat in the SUV once I got out of school, I probably should have gotten it over with, but I also knew I couldn't get rid of the guards who kept to the shadows wherever I went. Instead, I went home and told Arely to call off the men, so I could finally be a part of the society that had sealed our fate together.

"Fine, but you see Santi before you go and get an arsenal before you leave. I won't have you taking any chances."

Crossing the room, I enveloped her face with my hands and kissed her raw. Her body crashed into mine as her arms wound around my waist, pulling me closer as if she could defy physics and make us into one being. We broke away, panting, breathing in each other's air. I rested my forehead to hers as I spoke. "I would never do anything to purposefully leave you. I'll be back before you know it."

"I'm going to hold you to it." Her fingers traced the contours of my face, her eyes following after them before she nodded and took a step back.

I thought she'd follow me out of the room, but Arely stood where I left her, her eyes distant when I looked back at her before slipping out into the hallway and down the stairs to where Santi's office was.

The door was open like it always was. Still, I rapped on the door frame before I stepped inside. Santi's eyes shot up to meet mine. "Is everything okay?"

"As far as I know. I've got to get outfitted. I'm…" I pulled the parchment out of my pocket and waved it in the air, the wax seal gleaming in the light.

"Say nothing further. I'll make sure you're fully prepared for whatever comes your way. Although, I'm surprised you haven't opened it up yet."

"It's killing me not to, but I needed to do this, and I didn't want anyone trying to talk me out of whatever it is I have to do."

"You'll do perfectly. I am sure they won't ask you to kill anyone, so it should be plenty simple. Although whatever it is will be for their gain, make no mistake about that. It will most definitely be something illegal."

"I have no problem with that."

"If you did, you wouldn't be here." Santi stood and strode over to the wall. He pushed on one of the books until the wall opened up to a secret passage.

"Are there more of those through the house?"

"Wouldn't you like to know?" he chuckled. "Ask my

sister when you get back. Now let's outfit you with as many weapons as we can without it being obvious you're armed."

"Do you think they'll be watching me?" Like they did the night I was sent for Arely.

Santi's eyes flicked to mine. "I can't say, but I wouldn't put it past them. Just be careful. Their tests are always dangerous because they want you to prove your worth. You'll do fine. Maybe not before you met us, but now…" he smirked as if he was responsible for me being able to defend myself.

Pulling open a drawer, Santi picked out two knives and set them on the counter in the middle of the armory before he went to the wall and studied the guns. "Which are you most comfortable with?"

"I have the 9 mil I always carry." I looked at the wall filled with guns. They were mostly handguns, but there were some rifles and semi-automatics—not that I'd be needing them. "Do you have a holster where I could put one at my ankle?"

"Smart thinking, kid. Now I see what my sister sees in you," he chuckled as he went back to the counter and pulled out a Smith and Wesson 380 in a holster. "It's not forbidden to be armed, and I'm sure they're expecting it after your previous test, but it's best to have them hidden away. You'll do just fine."

Slipping the holster on, I tucked my jeans over it and put one of the knives in my sock on the other leg, and pocketed the other. Looking down, I couldn't see any noticeable bulges.

Santi looked me over before he closed the drawer and left the room. "Put your phone in the pocket with the knife. It will hide it better."

It occurred to me that this might be a trap to get to Arely once again. "Are you going to be extra vigilant about security while I'm gone?"

"No doubt. They won't be hitting us unaware. Don't worry about us. You focus on your task at hand."

I wasn't sure if it was possible not to worry about Arely when I was gone. When I was at school, my mind was always drifting to thoughts of her and her safety, even though I knew she always had a team of people to protect her.

Always being on guard was something I was used to, but worrying about someone else's welfare was entirely new to me.

Waiting until I was outside of the compound, I pulled the test out of my pocket and read what I was tasked with doing for the first time.

2410 South Hickman

Get the footage in the basement dating for the last year.
Drop it off in the trashcan on the corner of Stein and Lubbock by
midnight.

SIMPLE ENOUGH. It was almost as if they knew of my pickpocket ways before I fell in with the Guerreras. Stealing was in my wheelhouse. Killing people who were not trying to kill the ones I care about or myself was not. I could do this with my eyes closed. I would have liked to scope the place out before I went in, but I didn't have that luxury.

Turning on my bike, I soared down the road that led into Stonewall, letting the wind clear my mind of everything else I had to accomplish tonight.

Rolling to a stop at the address given to me, I eyed the Mexican restaurant. What footage could they possibly have here that would be damning?

Whatever, I didn't care. I was going to complete my mission, drop it off at the location they wanted, and get the hell home to my woman.

After parking a block away, I walked the perimeter twice to get the lay of the land. There wasn't a door that led directly to the basement, so that meant I had to go through the restaurant, which wasn't ideal, but I'd manage. I was lucky I had my tools so I could pick the lock. I didn't think breaking and entering a restaurant would be part of my test. I didn't spot a security system, which wasn't too smart on their part. Still, I kept my eyes open because if there was footage to be had, there were most likely cameras somewhere. At least in the basement.

Pulling my mask over my face, I walked to the back of the restaurant and quickly let myself inside the kitchen area. With my flashlight in hand, I went in search of a door that would lead downstairs. When I didn't find it, I headed into the seating area. The door wasn't easy to find. It wasn't meant for everyone to use, but I found it with two heavy-duty locks on it that were harder to pick than the previous one. Picking locks wasn't something I regularly did, so it took me some time. All the while, I had a time clock ticking down in my head. The footage I was supposed to get needed to get out of my hands by midnight at the latest. Otherwise, I was out.

I was sure Arely and the rest of the Guerrera family wouldn't care if I didn't pass the test, but the fact that no one could reassure me I wouldn't die if I didn't pass wasn't reassuring. If I lived, I didn't want Arely to have to keep part of her life hidden from me. This society they belonged to was a secret for a reason, and I already knew too much, which meant I'd probably be killed if I didn't pass.

Going downstairs, I was shocked to find a large room that was bare except for a couple of platforms with poles running through them. Definitely not what I was expecting. The closer I looked, I noticed booths lining one wall. Were there performances here? Was I sent on a task to keep an indiscretion out of the eyes of someone's wife? If so, this was the easiest fucking test ever.

I scoured the bottom floor looking for a door to a surveillance room but soon realized I wouldn't be able to see it with a blind eye after only finding a room filled with furniture. I set about knocking and pushing on the walls for a secret room where the footage might be hidden.

If I could have pulled my hair out by the root, I would have. Frustration was mounting as I tapped every inch of the last wall when I heard it. The sound was hollow. Fucking finally. I looked to see if there was anything that would trigger an opening but saw nothing but a plain black wall. Maybe I'd watched too many movies to expect something so obvious as a book to pull out or a sconce. I went about pushing where I thought the seam might be and was close to slamming my body into the wall when it finally gave in and slowly hissed open.

Now I just had to figure out where the last year of this place was. I was sure it wouldn't be neatly on one tape. That would be too easy. I wanted to pull out my phone and check the time, but I knew I'd already spent too much time searching, and seeing the little amount of time I had left would only make me reckless. I needed to keep my head in the game and get this shit done.

The room was small. It barely fit a desk inside with a chair. The wall with the desk pushed up against it was filled with monitors that were turned off. I hit the keyboard to bring the computer to life to find it needed a password. Each monitor mocked me to attempt to get inside. There was no way I was going to figure my way in when I had no idea who even owned the place. Instead, I focused on trying to find physical copies. Opening and closing drawers, I found a zipped binder full of DVDs. Each one had a month and year printed on them. This was too easy. Each disk was put in order by month and year, dating back three years. I was sure no one would notice the disks were missing until the next month when the next disk was added to the collection.

Was each disk a month's worth of surveillance?

It didn't matter to me what was on them as long as I didn't get caught. After pulling out all twelve disks, I looked for anything I could put them in. There was no way the pockets of my jeans or leather jacket would hold them all without them falling out. In the corner by the desk, I found a trash can that was empty of everything but a trash bag. Removing the bag, I placed the discs inside and tied the end.

Putting the binder back where I found it, I made sure it looked as if I hadn't been in the room. Walking back out into the large barren room, I wondered what went on here. I quickly shook my head, knowing I had no time to dwell on the matter. I needed to get out of here and drop these discs off. The only problem was I couldn't lock the door that led down. As soon as someone noticed the door was unlocked, they'd be hyper-alert an intruder had been in their midst. It didn't matter to me. By then, I'd be long gone.

It didn't take me long to get back to my bike, which I'd parked down the block. While I didn't see any cameras on the outside of the restaurant, I wouldn't be surprised if there were some. The security might seem lax, but I had a feeling it was all for show. They'd know the figure who walked by more than once was likely the one who broke in, but there was no way in hell anyone would know it was me except for the one who sent me here in the first place.

Rolling my mask up to the top of my head, I took in my first breath of fresh air in what felt like hours. After a couple of deep inhales, I pulled on my helmet and set off to the corner of Lubbock and Stein. I was so ready to get back to Arely and into our bed. I was always horny as fuck after a successful job and now was no different.

I still wasn't used to calling her house ours. I didn't even move my things in. I woke up after being stabbed, and all my clothes were hanging in her closet. I didn't fight her on it, though. It wasn't like I wanted to spend time away from Arely.

Five minutes later, I was driving away from the trash can where I was instructed to drop off the information and headed back to the Guerrera compound to fuck my woman.

And just like that, I was part of a society that might have planned to kill the love of my life. I vowed there and then that I would do everything in my power to find out who was behind sending me to murder Arely.

arely

"YOU OWN THIS PLACE?" Sebastian said from my right side as we stepped inside the restaurant.

"Yes, we do. We have to have some legal businesses. Otherwise, the government would be all over us," I quietly said as we passed a table.

"Makes sense."

Out of the corner of my eye, I watched him take in the surrounding room. I wondered what he was thinking after the other night.

"This is nice and smells damn good." He placed his hand over his stomach and smiled. "It's making me hungry."

It had been far too long since we'd last been here. Maybe we should start having our family dinners here and our meetings downstairs. The only way we could do that was if Army's fake little girlfriend wasn't in attendance.

We walked past a mural of the desert and into the room that was set up for us. The tablecloth was white with multi-colored dishes set in front of each chair. Wine and water glasses sat to the right of each plate with a big, colorful flower centerpiece in the middle of the table.

"If there's anything else you need, Ms. Guerrera, please let us know," the hostess said before she scurried out of the room.

Sebastian chuckled next to me.

"She usually has to deal with Pablo," I said as an explanation, which was enough.

"And there's a whole other level?"

"Down below. It only happens once a month. If the authorities came in, we don't want them to find anything."

"Why have it here at all?"

He was right, and he had no idea what happened downstairs once a month. We should have it in a separate location altogether, but no one wanted to travel miles out of town for their debauchery. After all that transpired in the last few months, I need to have Pablo start looking for another location for us to buy under a dummy company.

"We should change it." I sat down in my seat at the head of the table. "I've been too busy with other things and haven't been here in so long the entire thing hadn't crossed my mind." I smiled over at him as he sat in the seat beside me. "Thanks for looking out for us."

"Always." He bent down to kiss me but was interrupted when the door flew open, and Santi stepped inside.

Santi had a mischievous grin on his face as he looked over at us. "Oh, tonight is going to be a good night, Sebastian boy. You have no idea what we have in store for you."

Sebastian's eyes flicked back and forth between us before finally settling on me. "Why the surprise?"

"Because I want to see it through the eyes of someone who's never experienced it before."

Santi chuckled as he sat in his seat on the other side of me. "It will be priceless."

Leaning back into Sebastian, I laughed. "Are you nervous?"

"Never." He answered instantly, and I knew he meant it. I had a feeling he'd only been nervous when I was shot by the way he talked.

Santi looked to the door and back to me. "Where are the twins?"

"Your guess is as good as mine. They should be

here by now." Dread started to pit in my stomach. "Do you think they're okay?"

"Yeah, it's probably just Ale not wanting to go downstairs," Santi replied, looking over his shoulder at the door.

"Text them and see where they are," I ordered.

"I already did." He looked down at his phone and then back up to me. "The dots are jumping, so give them a minute. Ale is responding back."

My heart rate slowed, knowing Ale was okay. I knew if he was responding, then Army was safe as well.

"They're on their way. It took Army an hour to get rid of the 'girlfriend,'" he said with air quotes before laughing. "She may be DEA, but she's way too innocent to see what's going on downstairs."

Sebastian huffed and rolled his eyes. "Now you guys are just fucking with me."

Leaning over, I whispered against his ear, making sure my lips brushed against the shell of his ear. "I guess you'll just have to wait and find out."

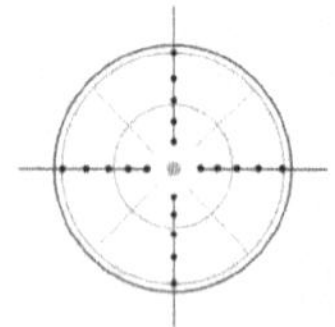

SITTING through dinner with my family was difficult when all I wanted to do was get downstairs. Everyone but me, Sebastian, and Santi left to do their own thing once dinner was over.

I couldn't keep my eyes off Sebastian as we took the stairs down to the party. I wanted to see his reaction once he saw what was going down. This was our monthly playtime with the Scorpio Society. I was sure there were other times between our parties they got together, but I had no interest in going to them unless it was required.

The second we hit the landing, I watched as his eyes widened for a brief second and then shot at me. "This happens every month?"

I nodded and turned to the room. It was full of people sitting on various couches and chairs. Two gorgeous and naked women danced on platforms with poles. For the most part, people were talking in their quiet circles, but in the back of the room, in the dark corners of booths, I knew what was transpiring there even if I couldn't see it.

"What do you think?"

"I think I'm going to like the Scorpio Society," he absentmindedly said as he scanned the room.

"Yes, it has its incentives." I curled around his arm and looked up at him with raised brows. "What do you say we go find ourselves a place to sit and have a drink while we watch the show?"

His eyes lit with intrigue as he moved through the room and scanned his surroundings. Once he found a chair that sat back away from the others, he pulled me down on his lap. "Arely," his voice trembled.

I twisted to look at him and saw the worry wash over his face before it was gone. "What is it?"

"My test."

Ah. For a brief second, I thought he wouldn't mention it, but I had no reason not to believe in Sebastian. He was loyal down to the marrow of his bones.

"What about it?" Gripping his hand, I traced his fingers with the tips of my own.

"They sent me to steal something. Discs. What was on them, I have no idea, but…" he swallowed, his throat clicking with the attempt, and looked back out to the room. "They sent me here. Down here. I had no idea you owned the place."

"Of course, you didn't. How could you? You'd never been here before." If he'd known it was our business, would he have still stolen the discs?

His face grew solemn as he flipped his hand over and clutched mine. "Have a damned you?"

"How so? There would be nothing on those tapes

to incriminate me except that it's in my place of business." My lips twitched. "How do you think you got in so easily? Do you think we have such shit security here that we'd let anyone break in and steal from us?"

"Knowing this is yours, no, but at the time, I had no idea. Now that I see what happens here, I can see why someone wouldn't want what they did for anyone to see."

"Oh, I can assure you no one sees what's on those discs, but they are even stupider than I thought if they think that was the only copy. Everything goes into the cloud. When we get home, we'll scour the meetings to figure out what they want to be hidden forever." I turned back around to look at the room while I tried to see if anyone was looking at us, giving away any hints as to who it might have been.

"Do you partake in the activities when you're here?" He breathed into my ear.

Was he wondering if I was on the video or any video? "I've been known to join in a time or two, but rest assured, nothing was caught on video. Do you want to join in the festivities?"

I felt him grow hard underneath me. His arms wrapped around my waist, pulling me even closer.

Wrapping his fist in my hair, he pulled my head back until I could see him out of the corner of my eye.

"I'm not sharing you with a single soul. Not now. Not ever."

"What about watching and maybe a little lap dance?" I circled my hips and ground down on his erection. "I want to show every one of these assholes the Guerrera queen has herself a king."

"Fuck, I like the sound of that." His hips bucked up and pressed his hard length into my core. His grip loosened on my hair, making it so I could move a little easier. I wanted to see his face, but listening to the way his breath quickened and his grip on my waist tightened was enough for now. There would be other times when I could see his face, even though this would be the first.

"Do you like to watch? Are you a voyeur, my queen?" He asked, panting.

"There's no harm in watching a little live entertainment. If you want, we can move closer. They won't mind. In fact, I think they like it." I arched my back and swiveled my hips.

"I'm not sure how long I'm going to be able to sit here with you grinding on my dick before I have to fuck you."

Arching my head back, I flicked his ear with my tongue. "You know, I wouldn't be opposed to moving someplace darker and riding your cock. Why do you think I wore this skirt tonight?"

"I don't think there could be a more perfect woman than you." He stood with me in his arms and sat me down. "Let's go have a look around." His hand skated down my back and cupped my ass before giving me a slap.

I laughed and laced our fingers together before I guided him toward a large bed where three couples were giving everyone a show. It was a tangled mess of one woman on her hands and knees while a man fucked her from behind, and she gave another man a blow job. Simultaneously, he had another woman on his face as he ate her out. While this scene was playing out, a man and woman roved their hands over and licked every inch of the four other bodies.

We stopped in front of the group of writhing bodies. Sebastian pulled me in front of him with one arm around draped over my collarbone, and the other pressed into my stomach. I felt his hot breath before I heard him. "When's the last time you participated in one of these?"

My body shook silently. "I've never been front and center. Having all of these assholes watch while I take my pleasure is not on my list. But if you must know, it's been at least a decade. Before you even knew what a hard-on was."

"Good," he pulled me tighter. "I guess I won't have to kill anyone then."

"I think you should keep talk of killing anyone in the society quiet. Everyone is a badass in their own right, and most have zero qualms in killing if they need to."

The sound of his throat clicking as he swallowed had me turning my head to look up at him. His face was a mask of indifference as he spoke. "I'm not sure if I'm ever going to be okay with them until I know with one hundred percent certainty that they had nothing to do with trying to kill you."

Pushing out of his grasp, my hand caught on his wrist and pulled him along, and I didn't stop until we were far enough away where no one could hear us. The second I was sure no one would overhear us, I spun around and narrowed my eyes at him. "Do you think I've given up on who tried to kill me? I know someone in the society had some sort of hand in trying to take me down. Trust me. When I find out who it was, I'm going to kill them after slowly torturing every last secret they hold. I will not give up, but I'm also not going to let them think I'm still looking into them. They gave you the easiest test known to the society, trying to placate me and the rest of my family, but they should know we will never forget."

"I shouldn't have said anything, but the thought of any one of these men touching you makes me want to burn down the world." Cupping my face with both of his hands, his eyes bored into mine. "And the thought that any one of these people tried to kill you has me wanting to bring on the apocalypse to make them feel exactly how I'd feel if anything ever happened to you."

Pushing up on my toes, I crashed my mouth into his as I pushed him further into the shadows and down onto the seat of one of the booths. My hands roamed over the planes of his chest, through his shirt, up the sides of his neck, and tangled my fingers into his hair as I swept my tongue along his.

Sebastian moaned into my mouth as his hands slipped underneath my skirt and cupped my bare ass. "Fuck, who knew me wanting to kill the world would be such a turn-on for you?" He chuckled as we broke apart and panted.

"I find it more than hot. The fact that you'd go to the ends of the world for me tells me more about how you feel about me than three simple words." I scrambled to undo his belt and pull his thick length out of his pants. The feel of velvet-covered steel filled my palm. I didn't waste any time as I placed his cock at my entrance and slowly started to sink down until I was fully seated. The way he stretched and filled me had me closing my eyes as I tried to soak in every ounce of pleasure and remember this moment.

"You're so fucking hot riding my dick and taking what you want," he groaned, cupping my breasts through my shirt.

I thought he'd watch the show behind us, but Sebastian never took his eyes off me. Bunching my skirt up in the front, he watched where we were connected, and, as impossible as it was, I felt him grow harder. The heat in his eyes burned bright, spurring me on. I rode him harder, slamming down on his length. Sebastian's hands moved to my hips and angled me in a way that had him rubbing against my g-spot with each stroke.

Pushing up my shirt until it was around my neck, he pushed down the cups of my bra until my breasts sprung free. His lips latched onto one nipple while the other plucked at the other. My core clenched around him as a wave of euphoria started to sweep over me.

"King," I gasped out as shudder after shudder wracked my body.

Letting go of my breast with a pop, he looked up at me, letting me see deep down into his soul.

"My Queen." Pushing his hips up, he stilled underneath me as I felt him pulse and swell deep inside of me. Groaning into the side of my neck, his fingers dug into the flesh at my hips as he held me still and unloaded inside of me. I knew I'd have bruises later, but I didn't care. I wanted something to help me remember tonight, even if only for a little while.

epilogue

Santi

MY SISTER and her boyfriend were so disgustingly in love it was annoying. They'd shown up tonight with matching crown tattoos on their ring fingers. I wasn't sure if that made them married or what. When I asked, they didn't answer. They only smiled at each other before they sat down at the table.

"Oh, good," Arely stood with a big smile on her face. "I wasn't sure if you'd make it or not."

Turning in my seat, I steeled my jaw as I saw Bree gliding toward the table with a sweet smile on her face.

"You know I never turn down an invitation to dinner." She hugged my sister and then sat down in the seat beside mine. "Hi, Santi," she said in the softest of murmurs.

"Bree." I tipped my chin in her direction and then stared off over Bash's shoulder, trying to focus on anything but the woman sitting next to me. The heat from her small body lapped at me in waves.

"Will the others be joining us?" Bree's voice was so sweet it nearly gave me a toothache.

"If they want to live, they will." Arely flashed a smile as if she was kidding. I mean, she wouldn't kill our brothers, but she would punish them if they didn't show up. That is unless they had a very good reason.

"Army's girlfriend." She could barely keep the sneer out of her tone as she said the word. "She likes to be difficult and make them late for *everything*. They need to start lying to her about the time so they can get here at the appropriate time."

I knew if Devi weren't an undercover agent, Arely would have demanded Army get rid of her. No, she wanted the girl to see we were a normal family and report back that nothing underhanded happened. Army was going crazy with his new role of being mentored by Pablo. He was to learn so he could take some of the weight off Pablo's shoulders, just as Ale and I were doing for Arely. It wasn't easy for her to give up control, but she wanted to spend more time with Bash and less time worrying about how shipments were doing and ways to expand our legitimate business to hide our other.

"Maybe they should just tell her how much you dislike people not being punctual. Surely the threat of you being angry with her would be enough to make her prompt," Bree giggled.

"Perhaps you're right. I will make my distaste for her lack of manners known once they show up. While we wait, why don't you tell me about the date you went on the other night? Was it a love match?" Arely laughed as if she knew it wasn't, but my heart was stuck in my throat. Bree went out on a date, and this was the first time I'd heard about it.

Bree stiffened next to me, and I could hear her swallowing down her nerves. "You know I have no interest in the men my father sets me up with. Eventually, he'll give up and realize I'm never going to get married," she said softly.

"Unless you find yourself in an arranged marriage. I see that happening before he ever thinks of you as unworthy of marriage."

I didn't know Bree's father personally, only professionally, but what Arely said had merit. I couldn't see Mr. Zee ever thinking his daughter was undesirable.

"I will never marry into a loveless marriage, and if my father ever tried to force me, I'd kill myself before letting it get that far."

"Bree," Arely gasped. "Don't say that."

"You don't know how some Chinese men treat their wives." She closed her eyes, hung her head, and shook it sadly. "Especially in arranged marriages. I will not be some concubine or servant just so my father can proudly say I'm married."

"No, I don't, but still, I won't let you kill yourself. I won't let your father marry you off either, but you've got to put yourself out there. Especially if he's pushing you." There was a pregnant pause before she asked. "What about the guy you like?"

Bree's head shot up and looked at me. "I never said—"

"In unspoken words, you did. I know you like someone, but you won't say who. Why not? Is he a horrible man I wouldn't approve of? Because really, I wouldn't care if it was the devil himself as long as he treated you well."

"I haven't… we haven't. It's not like that. He barely

knows I exist, let alone want to date and marry me." Bree blushed. Her shaky hand reached for her drink, only to knock it over.

I stood quickly and dashed out of the room to grab a few towels. I was back and drying up her water while I tried to process what Bree had said. I wanted to shout. I knew she existed. I would date her, marry her, and give her as many babies as she wanted, but all I could do was sit silently. I knew her father would never approve of me.

"Why don't you fake date someone to get his attention? If he sees you dating someone else and thinks you might be off the market, I bet he'll come running because I know there's no way in hell if you like this guy, he doesn't know you exist."

Bree rolled her eyes at my sister. "Just because you're happy doesn't mean that's a possibility for the rest of the world. I've accepted my fate."

"What about Santi? He could take you out on a few dates. Hell, maybe we could even go on a double date. You wouldn't mind, would you, Santi?"

All eyes were on me as I tried to swallow. Arely had no idea what she'd just suggested. I wasn't sure who this mysterious man was that Bree liked, but I was going to make her forget all about him. By the end of this faking dating arrangement, Bree Zee would only have eyes for me.

"I'm always happy to help out a friend," I smiled tightly. I didn't want to come across as too eager and let anyone figure out what I had in store for my sister's best friend. Bree Zee would soon be mine.

Did you enjoy KING'S VOW If so, please consider leaving a review on Goodreads, Amazon, or BookBub. Reviews mean the world to authors especially to authors who are starting out. You can help get your favorite books into the hands of new readers.
I'd appreciate your help in spreading the word and it will only take a moment to leave a quick review. It can be as short or as long as you like. Your review could be the deciding factor or whether or not someone else buys my book.

To stay up to date on all my releases subscribe to my newsletter.
https://view.flodesk.com/pages/
6104ad460475fa3dd9f250b0

acknowledgments

My family- your support means so much. Thank you for all of your encouragement and giving me the time to do what makes me happy.

Thank you **Bex** for making my story into a book.

Thank you **Casey** and **April** for inviting into this world and all of your support.

To all my **author friends**, you know who you are. Thank you for accepting me and making me feel welcome in this amazing community.

To **Wildfire Marketing Solutions and Catherine**, thank you for all your knowledge and for helping me make Away Game a success!

Lovers thank you for always being there.

To each and every **reader**, **reviewer**, and **blogger** - I would be nowhere without you. Thank you for taking a chance on an unknown author.

also by ella kade

Willow Bay Series - Forbidden Romance

Away Game - MM, Bully

First Down - Sister's Best Friend

Over Time - MM, Student/Teacher

Off Sides - Second Chance, Forbidden

Sin's Sacrifice - MC, Second Chance

www.ingramcontent.com/pod-product-compliance
Lightning Source LLC
Chambersburg PA
CBHW060912210726
48293CB00006B/2062